SUICIDE

OTHER BOOKS BY DOROTHY B. FRANCIS

COMPUTER CRIME

SHOPLIFTING
The Crime Everybody Pays For

VANDALISM
The Crime of Immaturity

SUICIDE

A Preventable Tragedy

Dorothy B. Francis

LODESTAR BOOKS   E. P. DUTTON   NEW YORK

The author and publisher gratefully acknowledge permission to reprint the article on pages 91–94: "To the graduates: Life isn't high school" by James P. Gannon. Copyright © 1986, Des Moines Register and Tribune Company. The article originally appeared in the *Des Moines Sunday Register* on June 1, 1986.

Copyright © 1989 by Dorothy B. Francis

All rights reserved. No part of this publication may be reproduced or transmitted in any form or by any means, electronic or mechanical, including photocopy, recording, or any information storage and retrieval system now known or to be invented, without permission in writing from the publisher, except by a reviewer who wishes to quote brief passages in connection with a review written for inclusion in a magazine, newspaper, or broadcast.

Library of Congress Cataloging-in-Publication Data
Francis, Dorothy Brenner.
  Suicide : a preventable tragedy.

  Bibliography: p.
  Includes index.
  Summary: Discusses who commits suicide and why, how to recognize warning signals, and what friends and family can do to prevent it.
    1. Suicide—United States—Prevention.
  2. Youth—United States—Suicidal behavior.
  [1. Suicide]   I. Title.
  HV6548.U5F66   1989   362.2   88-26856
  ISBN 0-525-67279-6

Published in the United States by
E. P. Dutton, a division of
Penguin Books USA Inc.

Published simultaneously in Canada by
Fitzhenry & Whiteside Limited, Toronto

Editor: Virginia Buckley

Printed in the U.S.A.   First Edition

10 9 8 7 6 5 4 3

for Richard

ACKNOWLEDGMENTS

I would like to extend warm thanks to the following people for their help in locating research material for this book: Virginia Buckley, Mary Christian, Carol Farley, James P. Gannon, Dr. Herbert Hendin, Kristi D. Holl, Linda Laventhall, Charlotte P. Ross, Lawrence M. Stewart, and Dee Stuart.

Contents

1. An Overview 3
2. Who Is the Potential Suicide? 11
3. Why? 20
4. Depression 33
5. Is Suicide Contagious? 41
6. The Warning Signs 49
7. One Girl's Story 57
8. One Boy's Story 65
9. How to Help Your Friend 73
10. How Schools Can Help 83
11. What's a Family to Do? 95
12. The Role of Church and Community 103
13. The National and International Scene 111
14. You Are Stronger Than You Think 116
    Reference Materials 123
    Index 127

SUICIDE

Youth suicide strikes at every level of society. Those we have already lost through suicide include the best and brightest of their generation. It is a national problem that can be solved only through the combined efforts of individuals, organizations, and government.

Charlotte P. Ross, Executive Director
Youth Suicide National Center

1

An Overview

Few people like to discuss suicide, and for years it has been considered a taboo subject. When such a subject exists, myths frequently spring up around it. This is true of suicide. Through the ages, many myths have been passed down from generation to generation, and these must be discarded before a clear look at the facts is possible. Today the first step on the road to better mental health may be the dispelling of false beliefs.

"Nothing could have stopped her once she decided to take her life." Have you heard that one? It's false, of course. Even hopelessly suicidal people have mixed emotions about death. Their minds can be changed if someone will take the time and effort to give them a push toward life.

"The person who fails the first time will eventually succeed." This is another oft-repeated myth. Facts point out that only 1 percent of suicide survivors kill themselves within a year, and only 10 percent within ten years. The suicide crisis is temporary. Of all attempters, 90 percent never try again.

One of the most dangerous myths is the belief that people who talk of killing themselves never do. False. They do.

"He's looking for attention. Just ignore him." Haven't you heard such comments? The first statement is true. The suicidal person is looking for attention—in the form of help. The second statement is the dangerous one. Don't ignore this person. Learn the ways in which you can give him the help he's seeking.

Many people believe that talking about suicide to a troubled person may give that person morbid ideas of taking his own life. This is false. He already has the ideas, and verbalizing them will help bring them into the open where help may be available. The danger lies in silence.

Have you been led to believe that people under a psychiatrist's or psychologist's care are out of danger and rarely take their lives? This is false. There is no guarantee that psychiatric treatment will help a troubled person. Such care is usually a step toward better mental health, but the suicidal patient also needs the listening ears of others who care for him.

People think that self-inflicted death often occurs with no previous warning. This, too, is a dangerous myth. The suicidal person usually gives many indications of his feelings.

It is also a myth that people who kill themselves are insane. Less than 10 percent are insane. They may be depressed or unhappy or neurotic, but few of them are insane.

The belief that the shame and embarrassment of an unsuccessful attempt will keep a person from making a second life-threatening attempt is false. Unless the cause of his pain decreases, a very troubled person may try again.

Most parents believe their children aren't likely to kill themselves. Most teenagers believe their friends aren't going to take their lives. The truth is that anyone can be suicidal, given the right circumstances and a depressed and hopeless frame of mind.

There's another age-old saying that suicide runs in families and that there's little anyone can do to prevent it. This belief holds some truth. Sometimes the desire to take one's life does seem to be an inherited tendency, but it is a fallacy to believe that nothing can be done to stop it.

If you've fallen for the line that most people who kill themselves are elderly, think again. Statistics show that in this country around six thousand young people die by their own hands every year. It is estimated that another six hundred thousand make a life-threatening attempt. These statistics are not exact because countless suicides and attempts go unreported.

Sometimes the police or medical officials cover up a self-murder to try to protect the surviving family from gossip. Frequently the reasons for nonreporting may involve money. If a death is self-induced, insurance payments may be voided. To give the family financial advantage, officials may report the tragedy as accidental.

Many times suicides and suicide attempts are unreported because the families lie about the true circumstances.

"He was cleaning the gun and it went off accidentally."

"He fell asleep at the wheel."

"He was sleepwalking when he fell from the window."

All of these explanations, plus many more, have been used to lessen family pain and embarrassment.

Webster's dictionary defines *suicide* as the act of taking one's life voluntarily and intentionally. Sigmund Freud, the founder of psychoanalysis, called self-inflicted death aggression turned inward. Many present-day mental-health workers define suicide as a cry for help. Whatever its definition, suicide can be prevented.

Not a minute passes in this country that someone doesn't attempt to take his life. Every ninety minutes, a teenager or young adult is successful in killing himself. The suicide rate for America's young people has tripled over the last thirty years. In 1978, the Centers for Disease Control in Atlanta announced a series of goals to reduce the number of deaths from motor vehicle accidents, suicides among young people, shootings, drownings, falls, home injuries, and fires. Now, ten years later, suicides of people ages fifteen to twenty-four is the only category for which the rate has not declined. Only accidents and homicides take more young peoples' lives than suicide.

Although these present-day statistics are alarming, self-murder is not a phenomenon of this century. Historical writings show it was a problem in ancient Greece. The philosophers Plato, Socrates, and Aristotle believed that to kill oneself was an offense against the state, because the destruction of useful citizens weakened the state economically.

The ancient Romans took a different view of self-inflicted death. To their thinking, to live nobly also meant to die nobly, even at a moment of personal choice. There were, it must be noted, exceptions to this belief. For instance, the purchase of a slave carried a money-back guarantee. If the slave killed himself within six months of purchase by his new master, the buyer was reimbursed. And a soldier who committed suicide was considered an unworthy deserter.

In ancient Rome, punishment for a crime frequently required forfeiture of the criminal's estate. An accused person, seeing that his family might thus be denied an inheritance, sometimes tried to avoid this situation by taking his life before his case came to trial. Once the Roman lawmakers made it illegal to commit suicide in order to avoid trial, to do so was considered to be without legal heirs, and a person's estate still went to the government. On one level, the Romans may have considered self-murder a noble act, but they also legislated against it.

Early Christian teachings brought new attitudes toward suicide. The first followers of Christ considered life on earth unimportant. They believed that the fuller the life, the greater the temptation to sin. Death and the promise of heaven, therefore, were a release sought with impatience. The ancient Romans may have fed Christ's followers to the lions for sport, but some of those victims saw the lions as instruments of glory and salvation. Thus Christian teaching was, at first, an inducement to self-inflicted death.

Posthumous glory was another incentive for self-killing, almost as powerful as the promise of heaven. Martyrs' names were celebrated annually in the church calendar, and martyrdom wiped out all transgressions. To die in this manner was a guarantee of paradise.

These beliefs lasted until the fourth century, when St. Augustine, a Christian teacher, convinced people that the sixth commandment—"Thou shalt not kill"—made suicide a sin. He believed that greatness of soul was proved by the ability to bear sufferings patiently.

In the year 533, as a result of St. Augustine's teachings, the Council of Orleans, the church's lawmaking body of that day, denied funeral rites to anyone who killed himself while accused of a crime. Thirty years later, the church denied funeral rites to all suicides, and in another thirty years, new church law ordained that those who attempted self-death would be excommunicated.

The suicide-as-sin theory prevailed for many centuries. In the 1600s, the body of a self-murdered victim was horse drawn to a place of punishment and shame. His body was hanged on a gibbet until a magistrate authorized its removal. A person who took his own life was considered as low as the worst criminal.

Sir William Blackstone, the English legal authority of the 1700s, wrote that the suicide's proper burial place was on the highway, with a stake driven through the body. Authorities usually chose a crossroads as the burial site and placed a stone on the victim's face. The stone and stake were intended to prevent the person's ghost from rising to haunt the living. Until the late 1800s, a person who killed himself was considered a felon, and his property reverted to the Crown.

In France, a person who died by his own hand was hanged by the feet, dragged through the streets, and then burned on the public garbage heap. His property was confiscated, and his memory defamed. These practices continued until the French Revolution in the late 1700s.

During the 1800s, the legal penalties for self-murder gradually dropped away. The families of successful attempters no longer found themselves disinherited and tainted with the suspicion of inherited insanity. They could bury their dead and grieve for them in the same way as any other family mourned a loss.

The legal situation was also becoming easier for the unsuccessful attempter. He no longer faced the gallows or prison, although he might be required to undergo a period of observation in a psychiatric ward. More often, the public, his friends, and his family left him to his continuing depression.

An Overview

Today many people consider self-inflicted death a personal matter rather than a mortal sin. It has become the subject of much scientific research, and there has been a steady growth in public concern.

While many people consider suicide a tragic event and a desperate act, others think differently. Some believe that there are circumstances in which self-willed death should be allowed. What about the elderly who hate burdening those who care for them? What about the terminally ill who abhor an artificially prolonged life?

There are cases where a doctor, upon request from the patient, induces the patient's death. This is called euthanasia. Another instance would be when somebody, at the request of an ailing person, helps that person to die. Many moral and legal questions arise whenever the subject of euthanasia presents itself.

You may say that no human has the right to take another life except in war, self-defense, or in legally administering capital punishment. What, then, is the difference between a hopelessly ill person who gives up on life and the youth who also wants to die? Both are feeling despair, hopelessness, and an alienation from family and friends. Whose need is greater? What is right and what is wrong in these circumstances?

These are hard questions, and they may never be answered to everyone's satisfaction. Some states are enacting right-to-die laws in an attempt to provide answers. These laws give an adult a constitutional right to refuse medical treatment, even though doing so may mean death.

There has been no law passed that gives a hopeless youth the right to take his own life. Few people can imagine the enactment of such a law. Instead, the suicidal young person is encouraged to seek professional help, and society is taking important steps to provide that help in ways that may save thousands of lives each year.

From this brief overview, it is apparent that attitudes concerning suicide have changed and are still changing. Families are becoming more aware of what their members may be thinking and feeling. Schools and communities are facing the subject of suicide with a will to do something to prevent it. Scientists are devoting more time and research to the matter. When everyone begins to work together, the incidence of self-inflicted death may become a thing of the past.

Suicide is a preventable tragedy.

2

Who Is the Potential Suicide?

Is it possible to draw a profile of the typical person under the age of twenty-four who may take his own life? If so, there are many things to be considered. Identifying a suicidal person may be the first step in preventing a tragedy.

Young women account for 15 percent of the nations' female suicides. Young men account for more than 20 percent of the male suicides. Young black males have the highest self-murder rate in our country, and the United States now has one of the highest self-inflicted death rates for young men in the world. It has surpassed Japan and Sweden, countries long identified with the problem of youthful self-destruction.

Where a person lives may in some way account for his or her life-taking tendencies. Certain states have a higher incidence of suicide than others, according to a 1985 report from the Centers for Disease Control in Atlanta. States with low suicide rates—seven to ten per 100,000 people—include Nebraska, Illinois, Mississippi, Indiana, South Carolina, New York, Massachusetts, Connecticut, and New Jersey.

Nevada has the highest incidence of suicide in the

nation, varying from nineteen to almost twenty-three per 100,000, and Arizona and New Mexico are close behind, with rates of sixteen to nineteen per 100,000. The high percentages in these western states may be due, in part, to the greater incidence of self-inflicted deaths among Native Americans. In the past twenty years, suicide among Native American adolescents has increased 200 to 300 percent.

Regardless of other factors, any person under undue stress is a candidate for suicide. The increase in self-murder among the young has gone hand in hand with a rise in other serious problems among this age group, such as drug and alcohol use, unwanted pregnancy, delinquency, and crime. When these problems occur in a young person's life, they create stressful situations that he may have difficulty in handling.

In 1966, statistical studies showed that a youth in danger of taking his own life was likely to have family problems. He might have been contending with an unwanted stepparent, an alcoholic parent, a parent involved in multiple marriages, a home situation that caused extreme conflicts, or a combination of these. Having a relative or close friend who had tried suicide also placed a young person at risk. Statisticians noted that 36 percent of suicidal youths were involved in a romance in its last stages, and that 22 percent of all female attempters either were pregnant or thought they were.

Now, twenty years later, many psychologists believe this information may still be a useful guideline in determining who is in danger of self-destruction.

It is sometimes impossible for a person to see into the private or home life of another individual. Often a youth doesn't know whether the members of his peer group come from families that are broken, stressed, or alcoholic. One can't always tell from looking at a girl if she is pregnant or if she fears she is.

The person inclined to take his own life is usually suffering from depression and hopelessness, and the symptoms of these afflictions can take many visible forms. Although it may be difficult for peers or adults to accurately pinpoint youths who are in danger, there are certain indicators.

Young people who attract attention to themselves, usually through their disturbing and disruptive behavior, may be feeling rejected by parents and peers. These young people may express their depression and their distress through reckless and outrageous actions. They become such a disturbance in the family or in the school that parents and teachers are forced to take action.

Everett Dulit, director of adolescent psychiatry at Albert Einstein Medical College in New York, believes that being outrageous is one of the pleasures of adolescence. In many cases, the outrageousness may be for theatrical effect, particularly on parents. But if a youth displays a real fascination with violence, destruction, or danger, then his outrageousness can point to serious problems.

Youths who take pleasure in drag racing their vehicles on public streets and highways may have subconscious suicidal tendencies. This may also be true of the aerialist who walks a cable above the Niagara gorge, the person who performs for video cameras by parachuting from a plane, or the human fly who seeks attention by climbing the outside of a skyscraper. Many psychologists believe that people with self-destructive tendencies deliberately choose jobs that place their lives in great risk.

Sometimes it is difficult for parents, teachers, or psychologists to determine when the attraction to excess is a cause for worry and when it is merely a part of normal growth. Frequently young people who act in especially dangerous ways are responding not so much to youthful exuberance as to depression. Their outrageousness is an attempt to escape the torpor and boredom that have settled over their lives.

Many young people flirt with danger or evil to show others they are growing up and leaving childhood behind. An incident or two of such behavior may not be a cause for concern, but repeated incidents should not be ignored, especially when they seem to be damaging other parts of a person's life, such as his progress in school or his basic health.

Youths who become involved in cult worship can be at high risk for suicide. By joining this group, they are displaying rebellion against traditional social values. Some cults persuade their young members to renounce parents as they worship a god who is living, wealthy, and authoritarian.

Many psychiatrists feel that the cult experience causes the adolescent to regress in behavior and thinking rather than to progress into maturity. Instead of preparing the youth to face the world, the cult strips him of decision-making opportunities. He is asked to surrender completely to the group leader. In this situation, the young person may become totally unable to face problems, to seek solutions, or to overcome depression. He has been placed at risk of suicide.

In 1988, a study reported in *Archives of General Psychiatry* suggests that adolescents who succeeded at suicide were more likely to have had firearms available in their homes than were other youths with suicidal tendencies. Guns are the young person's favorite suicide weapon. Each day of

1985, forty-five people in this country, some of them youths, used guns to kill themselves.

One boy who chose the gun was an A student and a high school football star from a rural Iowa town. Friends threw a party for this boy at age seventeen when he signed up to play football at a state university. At eighteen he put a gun to his head and pulled the trigger. Why? Nobody knows for sure, but friends speculate that it might have started with an injury that kept him on the bench instead of on the playing field. Surgery for the injury left him depressed, frustrated, and in pain.

Or maybe it was the steroids that he was injecting in the hope of speeding the healing process. Most likely it was depression and shame. This boy told his family that he felt he had let everyone down by being sidelined at the games. Whatever the cause, the gun was his way out, and it was readily available.

Another young football player who chose to die from a gunshot to the head was from Nebraska. He was an average student and applied much effort, self-discipline, and determination to everything he did. Friends called him an overachiever. His tactics for success worked for him in high school, but when he reached college, stresses became too great, and in spite of his willingness to work hard, he faced failure.

The loss of big college football money and the increasing pressures caused by the high expectations he placed on himself were some of the reasons given by family and friends for this boy's death. *Major reactive depression* was the term used by Dr. Kathryn Zerbe, a physician at the Karl Menninger School of Psychiatry in Topeka, Kansas.

Whatever the reason or the term, his solution was suicide—suicide with a readily available handgun.

The young person who is planning his own death may not be a boisterous, brawny football player who has easy access to a gun. He may not be one of the disruptive students in school. Instead, he may be that quiet person who almost blends in with the walls and who seldom says a word. Such people often make no emotional demands on anyone, but they can become depressed, withdrawn, and quietly preoccupied with death. In newspaper articles about young suicide victims, friends and family often comment that the deceased was "a nice, quiet person who never gave anybody a moment's trouble."

So now we are seeing that a potential suicide could be almost anyone. In addition to older youths, it could also be a very young child. It could be the six-year-old boy who deliberately ran into street traffic. In the hospital he told doctors he thought he would be in heaven and he was sorry he was still on earth.

Before taking his life, a nine-year-old boy wrote: "Mom, I got a bad note from school."

An eleven-year-old girl swallowed a full bottle of aspirin. After her rescue, she told her family she did it because she had lost her best friend and had nothing to live for. She made a second attempt several months later, and this time she succeeded.

A Des Moines social worker reported, "I've had kids as young as five show self-destructive tendencies. When a kindergartner gave me his teddy bear and asked me to keep it for him forever because he was going away for a long time, I knew he needed help."

A potential suicide may be a person of average intelligence or an academically gifted person. A 1986 survey of 2,631 adolescents aged twelve to eighteen who were randomly selected from public and private schools in a large Michigan county indicated that 8 percent of these students, anonymously questioned as to suicide intent, reported they had attempted suicide once during the previous year.

In 1986, another anonymous self-report survey of 385 students at a high school for the academically gifted in New York City found that 9 percent had made at least one suicide attempt sometime in their lives and that two-thirds of this group reported making two attempts.

Statisticians at the Metropolitan Life Insurance Company offer some insights into the problem of potential suicide victims as they divide suicides into three groups. People who are very seriously distressed comprise the first group, and they have every intention of solving their overwhelming problems in a final way.

About one-third of all suicides fall into this group. These people are determined to die, and they plan every detail leading to their demise with meticulous care. They allow little chance of failure. These people know exactly how they are going to accomplish their deaths, and they arrange to have the means available.

People in this category carefully select the time. They usually plan or write a final note, and they decide just where to place it so it will be easily seen. They may even consider who will discover their body. Boys are found in this category of attempters more often than girls. These people mean business—however, many of them are discovered in time to receive lifesaving treatment.

One Iowa high school boy who would be categorized in this first group was totally serious in his intent to do away with himself. He chose a day when his family was away. Thinking he would be alone for a long period of time, he drank a poison that he had brought into the house previously, and he fell unconscious. Luckily, family members arrived home unexpectedly, found him, and got him to a hospital in time to save his life.

The second group of people who attempt suicide are not really serious about ending their lives. They are crying for help in the form of attention, love, caring. They want someone to assist them in changing the horrible circumstances of their lives. Statistics show that more girls are found in this group than boys.

These attempters also plan their actions carefully, but their plans are designed to be lifesaving. They stage their try when family members are at home and readily available for help.

One California teenager, married to a young counselor and living in a family-care home for disturbed youths, slashed her wrists. With her husband and many of the resident youths nearby, she knew she was almost certain to be discovered in time to get help. Today she is alive and well on the West Coast.

The objective of those who try suicide with the hope of being saved is to manipulate the actions of others through their frightening behavior. If the person feels parents are too strict, the attempt may be an effort to achieve a relaxation of the rules. The attempter may also try to control a girlfriend or boyfriend by making the person feel guilty about the actions that have caused so much pain. Tragically, some of the people in this group die before help arrives.

The third group of people who attempt suicide are those who are confused and undecided about whether they want to live or die. They have serious problems that they cannot seem to solve alone and for which they cannot seem to find help. These people plan their deaths, but they don't plan carefully.

They might be compared to a person flipping a coin to decide the matter of living or dying. If they've planned their death so carelessly that help arrives, they'll be saved. If they've planned so well that they die, then that's how it will be. Actually, they're leaving the matter of their survival up to fate.

In a time of sudden anger and frustration, a Florida girl decided to end her life. She was alone in her home when she went to the family medicine cabinet and swallowed a few pills from the bottles there. She had no idea what kind of medicine she took or what physical reaction she might expect. Her living or dying was up to fate, and fate intervened in the form of family who returned home, found her, and summoned help.

Who is suicidal? We are still left with that big question.

A potential suicide victim can be anyone. The taking of one's life is an intensely personal act that occurs in all strata of society. There is no one typical suicidal youth. Perhaps the question of who commits suicide and who attempts to isn't as important in preventing this tragedy as learning the reasons behind the actions.

3

Why?

If there were an exact reply to the question of why young people commit suicide, it might be possible to put an immediate end to this self-destruction. But there is no single answer that will fit every incidence.

Birth factors may offer some clues. Sixty percent of teenagers who commit suicide have one or more of the following factors in their history: a mother who had no prenatal care for the first five months of her pregnancy; a mother who had a chronic disease during her pregnancy; an incidence of respiratory distress for more than one hour following birth.

Scientific researchers also are presenting convincing evidence that statistics concerning stress among people fifteen to twenty-four years old relate to their increasing percentage in the total national population. Because there are more young people, the rate of suicide among the young has increased.

While young people are powerless to control the varied circumstances of their birth, many of them have two traits in common. They want action right now, and they have trouble seeing into the future. Seldom do they dwell on the long-term results of their suicidal act.

Consequently, youths may take their own lives because they cannot imagine an end to their unhappy existence. It's probable that they've never seen anyone die and that they've never experienced great pain or even the death of a loved one.

Some young people may kill themselves because of a mistaken notion that it is a romantic thing to do. When parents try to thwart a relationship, what could be more romantic in the eyes of the frustrated lovers than to avoid parental restrictions by dying together? Or, if a girlfriend or boyfriend deserts a partner, the jilted one may consider suicide a dramatic means of quick revenge.

Such mistaken thoughts may have been going through the mind of a rural Iowa student who carried a gun to school, shot a classmate whom he believed did not return his romantic feelings, then turned the gun on himself.

A suicidal person sometimes acts in revenge against parents. One fourteen-year-old Midwestern boy rebelled because his parents asked him to stop spending so much time with his girlfriend. On the Friday before his death, he had been grounded for disobedience. The boy and his father had argued over the same issue on the morning he died. He waited until his parents went to church; then he loaded a gun, which was kept in the home, and fired a shot into his head. Revenge? On the surface, it would seem that was his motive. Deeper probing might unearth other causes.

Sometimes suicide in a youth may be an act of atonement. A sixteen-year-old boy in Alabama, whom we will call John, referred to himself as the man in his family. In truth, he was half man and half boy. He was man enough to lecture his sisters on gun safety, yet he was boy enough to play games with a handgun he carried casually in the glove compartment of his car.

One day while John was aiming his gun at a friend in play, the weapon accidentally fired, seriously wounding the other boy. John immediately tried to help his friend and apologized for what he had done. Later, when he was asked to leave the care of his friend to the paramedics, John did so. He walked to his car, took the gun, and shot himself dead.

Social isolation is another factor that can contribute to a youth's self-destruction. Almost three-fourths of the young people who make attempts on their lives have little or no social contact with others their own age. Such isolation can be devastating in a time of life when peers are very important. The loner may be terrified. He may be unable to communicate, and he may see death as the only solution.

Loss is another thing that can lead a young person to kill himself. The death of a loved one can thrust a youth into a state of depression, as can the loss of family love or the loss of attention, respect, or status among peers.

Some mental-health experts believe the high incidence of suicide among Native American youth may be related to the dissolution of their traditional life-styles, their low job skills, and minimal job availability. Stress caused by migrating from Indian land to large cities can also contribute to this tragedy.

Sigmund Freud believed that suicide is an act of hostility. His theory embraced the idea that the troubled person is killing someone he identifies with and someone he both loves and hates. In most cases, that person is a parent, and the child is killing the mother or father who exists within himself.

While some psychologists still consider Freud's theories

valid today, many question them. All children have parents who may inspire both love and hate, yet most youths do not commit suicide. All adolescents experience losses and stresses of various kinds. The question of why some are driven to suicide and some aren't remains a puzzle.

Is a tendency toward self-induced death inherited? Drs. Janice Egeland and James Sussex of the Psychiatry Department at the University of Miami School of Medicine have studied a population of the Old Order of Amish in southeastern Pennsylvania. They chose this segment of people to examine because their isolated and restrictive life-style protects them from factors often related to suicide potential in other Americans.

For example, since the Amish came to America in the early eighteenth century, they have had no known murders or serious criminal acts among their people. There is almost no instance of drug or alcohol abuse or unemployment. Their family structures are cohesive, and this reduces the chances of loneliness and isolation among the elderly, as well as hopelessness among all community members. Taking one's life is a taboo that is never forgiven by these intensely religious people.

Egeland and Sussex were able to verify twenty-six suicides in this Amish group between 1880 and 1980. These self-inflicted deaths clustered in four primary family groups. Seven appeared in one line, while five appeared in a second one. The latter family group also revealed two suspected suicides who could not be confirmed and who were thus omitted from the study.

Four of the Amish families in this study accounted for 73 percent of the suicides. These four groups, however, comprised only 16 percent of the community's total population. This study seems to show that sometimes tendencies toward self-destruction may be inherited. But the question remains: Why do these tendencies seem to run in some families and not in others?

In the summer of 1986, *Science Focus,* a publication of the New York Academy of Sciences, carried the following headline: Chemical Factor Found Among Causes of Suicide.

A study on suicidal behavior, cosponsored by the New York Academy of Sciences and the National Institute of Mental Health, has found that a deficiency in the brain chemical transmitter serotonin has been identified as a potential cause of self-inflicted deaths.

This study was corroborated by Dr. Marie Asberg of the Karolinska Institute in Stockholm, Sweden. She reported that 40 percent of a group of depressed patients she studied who had below-normal levels of 5-hydroxyindoleacetic acid (5-HIAA), the major breakdown product of serotonin, had attempted to take their lives. In contrast, the self-death rate among those in the same depressed group with normal levels of 5-HIAA was only 15 percent.

Another study, also in Sweden, showed that patients with low levels of serotonin—a brain chemical linked to mood and appetite—who had attempted self-destruction were ten times more likely to have died by their own hands than were those with normal levels. These studies seem to indicate that reduced serotonin may be a biochemical marker for suicidal and aggressive behaviors. If these findings are confirmed, it would be the first instance in the study of suicide showing a close tie between a specific biological finding and a specific pattern of behavior.

But still more questions arise. Some of the experts at this meeting of scientists have vowed to determine whether lower levels of serotonin are a cause or an effect of depression, a mental disorder closely linked to suicide. Other researchers want to learn if there is a relationship between alcohol use and low levels of this chemical. The search for answers continues.

Dr. John Mann, psychiatrist at New York Hospital–Cornell University Medical Center in New York City, and Dr. Michael Stanley of Columbia University reported at the 1987 annual meeting of the American Psychiatric Association that the brains of suicide victims show significant physical abnormalities that provide good evidence of an inherited tendency to commit suicide.

The researchers found that the suicide victims' brains contained fewer release sites for serotonin and more sites to receive serotonin than did the brains of normal subjects. This research strengthens the theory that the serotonin system is related to self-murder, but the doctors pointed out that it was unlikely that this abnormality was the only one to be found in such victims. They emphasized the importance of psychological factors and that a physical tendency toward self-destruction does not mean it is inevitable.

Research done in 1988 by Dr. Guy Goodwin of Littlemore Hospital in Oxford, England, shows that losing weight can alter the mind as well as the body. Goodwin saw a change in levels of serotonin.

In 1988, Dr. Neal Ryan, assistant professor of psychiatry at the University of Pittsburgh, reported at the American Psychiatric Association's annual conference in Montreal on his suicide study. His research, which focused on growth hormones in the brain, demonstrates neurochemical abnormalities in suicidal adolescents. Ryan also pointed out that there are environmental phenomena that impinge on the neurochemical abnormalities and that his findings in this study could help doctors identify and treat certain patients before they make a suicide attempt.

The study of chemical abnormalities of the brain is in its infancy. It is hoped that future research will demonstrate ways in which the incidence of self-inflicted death may be prevented.

In 1979, sociology professor David Phillips of the University of California at San Diego learned that media coverage of suicides tended to stimulate others to acts of self-destruction. He investigated the belief that some fatal traffic accidents may be caused by people who have decided to take their own lives.

Phillips checked Los Angeles traffic records for periods immediately following locally publicized suicides, and he discovered that for the three days following such reports in the *Los Angeles Times,* auto fatalities increased by 31 percent.

Later he found similar surges in Detroit, following front-page coverage of a self-inflicted death. Although it was impossible for him to prove that the increased auto deaths were intentional rather than accidental, he did note that in the three-day period following the news report, there was a higher-than-usual proportion of single-car accidents, the type of crash in which a potential suicide would likely be involved.

Phillips also noted that in the three days following a suicide report, the ages of the people killed on the road were close to the ages of the suicide victims. In addition, he found that the longer such a story remained in the news, the higher the national suicide rate climbed. Other interesting studies showed a drop in self-inflicted deaths in cities experiencing extended newspaper strikes.

Professor Phillips continued his studies, and in the mid-1980s he began drawing definite conclusions from them. In 1986, he and sociologist Lundie L. Carstensen reported in the *New England Journal of Medicine* that both movies and television news coverage of self-inflicted death tend to trigger a temporary increase in the number of teenagers who kill themselves. The increase, they say, is proportional to the amount of network coverage.

These researchers studied self-death rates in the week following thirty-eight stories or pairs of stories that appeared on the three networks between 1973 and 1979. The accounts of actual suicides covered a wide spectrum of victims, including television actor Freddie Prinze, an unknown teenage girl, and a man who had murdered several people. Documentaries included programs on suicide and teenagers, and suicide and prison.

On the average, in the week following a single suicide story, there were about three more self-inflicted deaths than would normally have been expected. Girls seemed to be more affected by the television programs than boys, and their suicide rate rose by 13 percent, while the rise for boys was 5 percent.

Another research team, Madelyn S. Gould and David Shaffer of Columbia University in New York City, followed suicide rates in the greater New York area two weeks before and two weeks after four television movies on suicide, which appeared in 1984 and 1985. Compared with the number of self-inflicted deaths predicted, an excess of six occurred after three of the broadcasts. No excess occurred after the fourth broadcast. When these figures are projected nationwide, they reveal in excess of about eighty self-induced deaths in young people ten to nineteen years old.

Upon seeing these reported statistics, officials at the three major networks criticized one or both of the studies, lambasting the researchers' conclusions and methodology. They also charged that the studies ignored the positive effects of the broadcasts, such as increased use of crisis hot lines and counseling services.

The information concerning media suicide coverage and the rise in suicide rates seems very discouraging at first glance. When it was released, news editorials appeared almost immediately, asking if such media coverage should be limited. Those opposed to this suggestion pointed out that these two studies were unable to identify whether the teenagers who killed themselves actually had seen the television shows in question.

There is reason to hope that the rise in self-inflicted deaths following media coverage of the subject can be curbed, and that such coverage can act as a deterrent to self-destruction. In the Gould/Shaffer study, the one movie not linked to an increase in the suicide rate focused sharply on the reactions of the surviving family members. It also included educational information about suicide prevention and about hot lines that people could call to get immediate help with their problems. The program left the clear message that there were many options open to troubled people other than death.

In a 1984 television drama about suicide, "Silence of the Heart," the parents of a boy who killed himself talk the victim's best friend out of jumping off a cliff. After this show, crisis hot lines in many cities were swamped with calls. The film's director, Richard Michaels, commented: "My number-one purpose is to communicate to young people who are deeply depressed or feeling suicidal that there are people who really care, and places they can go for help." Michaels wished to emphasize the fact that caring people are only a hot line call away.

Another theory on why young people kill themselves appears in the 1986 book *Schools Without Drugs,* printed by the United States Department of Education. This publication contains the following statements: Over time, drug use heightens bad feelings and can leave the user suicidal. More than half of all adolescent suicides are drug related.

Concern about young people and drugs has been growing in recent years. A recent Gallup Poll found that for the first time in almost two decades, American citizens have ranked drug use by students as the biggest problem facing school systems.

In the 1960s, the drugs making headlines throughout the nation were marijuana and LSD. In the 1970s, people were calling angel dust the family nightmare. In the early 1980s, cocaine topped the list of sought-after drugs; and now, in the late 1980s, the new substance alarming parents, teachers, and law-enforcement officers is crack, a cocaine derivative that is cheap, smokable, and easily obtained. This popular new drug spread from coast to coast in less than six months.

There's more. In 1987, basuco, a crude and cheap form of cocaine, appeared on the drug scene in the United States. This coffee-colored paste, long used in South American countries, has now found its way into Florida. United States Drug Enforcement Administration statistics indicate that basuco is not yet a big problem in the United States but that it needs to be monitored. It has the potential to outpace crack in terms of popularity.

Basuco is the cheapest form of cocaine, and at a dollar a dose, it is affordable for everyone. It is especially dangerous because it contains poisonous impurities such as lead and sulfuric acid, which can lead to serious brain damage, physical disintegration, and death. Basuco is yet another threat to the physical and mental health of the youth of our country.

No parent, teacher, or community member wants to see young people using drugs—especially drugs that may induce suicide—but drug-use statistics are frightening. One in sixteen high school seniors drinks alcohol daily, and 41 percent use alcohol regularly. The average age for starting chemical use is now between eleven and fourteen. Drug use has reached the elementary school level.

Psychologists report that it takes five to fifteen years of heavy drinking for an adult to become an alcoholic; it takes only six to eighteen months of such drinking for an adolescent to become addicted. The use of alcohol and/or other drugs is the number-one cause of successful suicides in the United States, according to the Drug Abuse Warning Network.

Dr. Richard Fowler of the University of California at San Diego reports that more than half of the under-thirty suicides in a San Diego area study were diagnosed as primarily caused by drug addiction or alcoholism rather than another underlying mental illness. Substance abuse was a secondary factor in another 13 percent of the deaths.

"Our data suggest that suicide is really a consequence of the drug use itself," Dr. Fowler says. "The disease process of alcoholism and drug use runs its natural course, and suicide is just one of the logical consequences. It's clear that the most important thing we can do to lower the suicide rate in young people is to intervene early when drug use is suspected."

Results of a recent study at The University of Iowa College of Medicine indicate that tendencies toward drug abuse may be passed on genetically from parent to child. The study of 443 adults given up for adoption shortly after birth found that a significant percentage of those who used drugs had a biologic parent who abused alcohol, a clue that a tendency toward substance abuse may be hereditary.

Researchers believe this study is important because it helps identify people who are at risk due to genetic factors. As a result of these studies, those people can be targeted for preventive efforts. Other studies have examined adoptees for a possible genetic link with alcoholism, but the Iowa study is the first in which the adoptees were used to determine whether other kinds of drug use are hereditary.

While scientists conduct experiments and engage in research looking for scientific causes of suicide, many parents, teachers, and other concerned individuals wonder if listening to certain kinds of music might cause a young person to take his life. The parents of a nineteen-year-old boy in California instigated a lawsuit claiming that the lyrics to a popular rock song led their son to shoot himself. A Los Angeles superior court judge rejected their assertions and dismissed the suit.

The idea that a type of rock music—heavy metal—may be a negative influence on youthful listeners was explored in 1987 on a segment of "20/20." Critics of heavy metal suggest that the loud, raucous music, with its screeching guitars and questionable lyrics, may incite suicide. It was pointed out that four recent suicide victims in Bergenfield, New Jersey, were heavy metal fans.

People who like heavy metal say that it speaks to the anger and despair of many teens today, and that without it as an escape valve, there might be even more incidences of self-inflicted death. These people also believe that the heavy metal listeners may be telling society how they feel about their lives. It is hostile music for hostile kids, and it matters because kids matter.

Acquired immune deficiency syndrome, more commonly called AIDS, is a disease that doctors think may be causing incidences of suicide. Scattered reports of AIDS-related suicides and suicide attempts are emerging across the nation, and health authorities fear such problems may become more common as the deadly disease infects increasing numbers of people. At this time the disease is so new that suicide-related statistics are unavailable.

No matter what form unhappiness takes, teenagers and young adults are often inexperienced in dealing with it. They have yet to learn that nothing lasts forever, that as dreadful as they feel at the moment, those feelings will come to an end. From the standpoint of their inexperience, it's easy for them to convince themselves that no other person in the world has ever felt as terrible as they feel. They see no solutions. It is sometimes easy for the troubled person in such a frame of mind to mistakenly view death as the only exit from his pain.

Whether suicidal feelings are sparked by immature impulsiveness, by inherited tendencies, by the lack of certain chemicals in the brain, by media coverage, by substance abuse, by disease, or by music, one great and fundamental cause underlying most of these causes is depression.

4

Depression

Psychiatrists describe depression as a condition of general emotional dejection and withdrawal—sadness greater and more prolonged than that warranted by any objective reason.

In the 1960s, psychiatrists tended to believe that only middle-aged or old people suffered from depression. They seldom associated the malady with children or young adults. Today doctors know that even babies can become so depressed that they stop eating. Researchers for the National Institute of Mental Health in Bethesda, Maryland, estimate that one in five young people may suffer from depression. Many doctors agree that this illness is undoubtedly the single most common and fundamental cause of childhood and teen suicide.

The intensity of this illness can vary greatly in different people. Teenagers and young adults tend to live spontaneously and to act on impulse, and many times their actions are triggered by pressures from parents, peers, school, and social environment. If the pressure a youth feels is great enough, it may lead to temporary periods of mild anxiety and depression.

Most teenagers have experienced feelings of sadness and discouragement now and then. A girl whose boyfriend has stood her up for their Saturday-night date may experience such feelings for a short time. After that, something may happen that cheers her up. Maybe her boyfriend presents a legitimate excuse for his actions, or maybe she finds a new boyfriend whom she likes better. In either case, the girl's sad feelings disappear, and after a short time she is cheerful again.

Some young adults may feel so unhappy that they are always ready to cry, even over minor incidents such as scoldings from a parent or teasing by friends. If asked, the unhappy people may be unable to tell you just why they are crying. Doctors call these sad feelings depression. An athlete forced to sit on the bench because of an injury may feel depressed until the season ends, but his inability to adapt to circumstances may return later if he faces another disappointing situation.

In some teenagers' lives, something always seems to be going wrong. One high school wrestler became gloomy when he found his car had a flat tire, which made him late for school. Then he weighed in too heavy, and the coach ordered him to do laps around the track in order to lose a couple of pounds. One thing led to another, day after day, until he began to lose his self-confidence and to think that life might never go well for him. Such temporary loss of hope and feelings of worthlessness are serious, but they are not considered a major depression.

Sometimes people experience mild cases of depression during winter months. For them, the change in seasons brings on sluggish and melancholy feelings. Dr. Norman E. Rosenthal, director of the psychobiology section at the National Institute of Mental Health, reported in a study published in the February 1985 *American Journal of Psychiatry* that the symptoms of winter depression decreased markedly in thirteen patients who were exposed to bright fluorescent lights for several hours each day in the mornings and evenings.

Since that time, experts from the National Institute of Mental Health have used light therapy on more than one hundred patients, and it has been effective for about 80 percent of them. The therapy, however, must be maintained throughout the winter. When it is stopped, depression quickly returns.

The purpose of the lights is to turn a winter-length day into a summer-length day. For the treatment to work, the lights must come from full-spectrum bulbs, like those used to grow plants. Studies have shown that dim fluorescent lights, such as those in homes and offices, do not produce the same beneficial results. Dr. Rosenthal says that it takes about one week for the therapy to produce results.

But what about the deeply dejected person? When mental-health experts speak of a major depression, they are describing more than just sadness. A person in such a serious mental state will show other symptoms of his illness. He may have trouble sleeping. He may be bored. He may lack energy. He may be irritable and have negative feelings about himself. These symptoms, in addition to feelings of sadness, add up to the clinical depression that is a mental disorder.

Young people may be confused by definitions of depression. How can they tell when their sadness calls for professional treatment?

As a general rule, doctors usually feel that an adolescent who continues to have gloomy feelings for longer than two weeks is showing symptoms of more than normal adolescent moodiness and may be suffering from a clinical depression. However, people who are able to continue with the regular routine of their lives, even though they are sad and lack confidence, are not suffering a major depression.

Some scientific researchers believe that the seriousness of suicidal intent correlates less with the degree of depression than with one particular aspect of the illness—hopelessness about the future. High suicidal intent has been observed in patients who showed minimal depression but whose expectations for the future were slight.

So, as we ask why young people take their own lives, we must also ask why the lives of some people seem so hopeless to them. And as we search for answers, we should remember that not all depressed people kill themselves, and that some who are not depressed do.

There may be as many reasons for depression as there are people who feel depressed. When a person experiences a loss, sad feelings may cause disabling symptoms. A loved one may have died. A parent may have left home. A friend may have moved away. Or the young person may have lost status with his friends or failed an important test.

It would seem normal for a person to grieve after any of these events, especially those involving the death of a loved one. To help differentiate between grief and a clinical illness, mental-health experts point out that a mourner's thoughts concern the lost person, while the depressed person's thoughts concern his own feelings of loss and guilt.

Sometimes the negative feelings of a bereaved person are a result of anger felt toward the deceased. Since the person considers these hostile feelings unacceptable, he cannot admit they exist. In dealing with the guilt generated by his angry feelings, he redirects the hostility toward himself. The result may be his self-inflicted death.

Depression is a malady that wears many masks. The student who drops out of high school, the girl who faces an unwanted pregnancy, the youth who is crippled as a result of taking an unreasonable risk—all may have been suffering from depression.

Pressure and stress may lead to dejection and suicide. Today's young people are under a great deal of parental pressure to succeed in school. In many affluent communities, grades are the only thing that can't be bought, so parents try to add luster to their own status by pushing their children to attain a straight-A average. Also, the competition for college acceptance sometimes plays a large role in putting a student under undue pressure to earn high grades.

The pressure of achieving top grades becomes very real when students lack an understanding of long-range educational goals. The final grade and the report card may be the only things some youths really comprehend. To them, anything but top grades is unacceptable.

Many young people also feel pressures at school resulting from meaningless comparisons. These pressures are usually social or athletic, and often they are self-imposed. Youths may feel a need to be chosen for a ball team or to belong to a group of peers. To be excluded can mark them as failures in their own minds. Or if they are a member of a team, they may feel that winning is their only option.

Such thinking may have passed through the mind of a North Carolina college student and champion runner. In a relay that she considered very important, she fell behind her competitors. When she reached a curve in the track, she kept running straight ahead, off the track and into the stands. Then she disappeared.

Few spectators noticed that she had left the race, but her mother was there and she summoned the campus police. The girl was later found lying in a marsh under the bridge from which she had jumped. She lived, but the doctor's prognosis was that she would be permanently paralyzed and unable to run again.

People who are under more stress than they can handle become afraid. They feel alone and worthless. They feel neglected and misunderstood. There is a lack of purpose in their lives. But most important of all, they carry in their minds a hopeless certainty that things will never get better.

Such feelings of hopelessness may have triggered the death of a thirteen-year-old California boy who was distressed over his family's financial problems. In his suicide note he wrote that he was hanging himself so his parents would have one less mouth to feed.

The good news for the depressed person is that life can get better. Clinical depression is one form of mental illness that responds to treatment that is readily available. When questions arise as to why a young person took his life, the answer is sometimes because that person and his family didn't actively seek help.

School guidance counselors and clergymen are there to assist those in need. Treatment also is available from various health professionals, psychiatrists, psychologists, and family doctors.

It is important for both the troubled youth and his family to engage a therapist in whom they have confidence and respect. If a patient doesn't feel at ease with his therapist, he should try again with another doctor—and again, if necessary. But once a patient has found a therapist who inspires confidence and respect, he should stick with him through the good times and the not-so-good times. In this way, real change for the better can take place.

More good news for the depressed person lies in the fact that each day scientists are working to discover more about depression and its causes. Many questions still remain as to why some people become depressed at certain life situations, while others do not.

In conjunction with her scientific studies concerning inherited suicidal tendencies, Dr. Egeland reports in a 1987 issue of *Nature* that she and her colleagues have discovered the first proof that some forms of depression are inherited because of a dominant defective gene. This means that people who inherit that defective gene from either parent will have a strong predisposition to the illness.

Although the location of the defective gene has been identified, the specific segment of DNA (the substance from which genes are made) has yet to be studied. When such studies are done, scientists will be able to learn what chemical processes in the brain go awry. It is hoped that these findings will be valuable in predicting who may develop clinical depression, in diagnosing it, and in allowing for more precise treatment.

At the annual meeting of the American Psychiatric Association in 1987, doctors reported finding that certain immune cells called lymphocytes may mimic brain-cell defects in some patients with depression. This suggests that the immune system and the brain share common chemical characteristics. The advantage of finding parallel defects in lymphocytes and brain cells is that lymphocytes can be easily obtained in a blood sample, while brain tissue is difficult and risky to obtain. Thus, lymphocytes may one day serve as the means to diagnose and determine treatment for psychiatric disorders such as depression.

The whys of depression and suicide are many and varied, but help is available to those who search for it.

5

Is Suicide Contagious?

Cheyenne, Wyoming, 1982: Three teenagers committed suicide in April.

North Salem, New York, 1983: Two teens killed themselves during a three-week period.

Westchester, Rockland, and Putnam Counties, New York, 1984: A string of twelve self-inflicted deaths shook communities.

Clear Lake City, Texas, 1984: Six young adults took their lives in less than three months.

Storm Lake, Iowa, 1984: Three teenagers committed suicide between May and December.

Spencer, Massachusetts, 1986: One boy killed himself, and four others made attempts.

Omaha, Nebraska, 1986: Three teens took their lives in a five-day period, and four others attempted to do so.

Manchester, Iowa, 1987: Two ninth-graders took their lives during a two-week period.

Richardson, Texas, 1988: Two high school students, one junior high student, and one elementary school student took their lives between February and May.

How could this happen?

Throughout the nation, we continue to ask ourselves this question. In the spring of 1987, on a Wednesday in March, four teenagers, ages sixteen to nineteen, were found dead of carbon monoxide poisoning in a car parked in an apartment complex garage in Bergenfield, New Jersey.

On Friday of the same week, two more teenagers, ages seventeen and nineteen, were found dead in a garage in Alsip, Illinois, a Chicago suburb. One day after that, a fourteen-year-old boy was found dead on the hood of a car in another Chicago suburb. His family found newspaper clippings about the Bergenfield and Alsip suicides under his bed.

That wasn't all. After another three days, a twenty-year-old woman and her seventeen-year-old boyfriend were found dazed after a carbon monoxide suicide attempt in the same garage where the first four teenagers had died. Four other carbon monoxide suicides took place in New Jersey, Illinois, Nebraska, and Washington in that same week.

The nation once again became aware of cluster suicides, a phenomenon of the 1980s. Ten years ago, if people had raised questions about suicide being contagious, researchers would have thought they were joking. This is no longer true.

"Suicide clusters probably occur much more frequently than we know about," says Dr. Mark Rosenberg of Atlanta's Centers for Disease Control. "Suicides generally tend to be underreported, in part due to concern about stigmatizing the deceased. Many such deaths are reported as accidents."

This may be what happened in the summer and early fall of 1986, concerning the deaths of four other Bergenfield youths. In June of that year, a freight train struck and killed one young man. It was August when another youth walked into a pond and drowned. In September a third boy died in a 200-foot fall from a cliff overlooking the Hudson River, and in that same month, a freight train killed another boy, who had talked to friends about suicide.

Officials later released information that showed that all four young men had been drunk at the time of their deaths. In the 1987 case involving Bergenfield youths, the four had taken cocaine in the two hours before their deaths, and the two boys were also found to have been intoxicated. In addition, it was noted that three of these youths were school dropouts and the other had recently been suspended from classes.

The 1986 tragedies were reported as accidents, but many people considered the possibility of suicide, especially when, a few months later, in the spring of 1987, they learned that one of the four carbon monoxide victims in Bergenfield had been a close friend of the boy who had died in a fall the previous September.

Again, the question of why this happened is hard to answer. To date, cluster suicides follow no set pattern. There is much debate among mental-health specialists over whether some of these deaths are part of a chain reaction or are coincidental. Many questions remain unanswered as experts study the facts.

In Clear Lake City, Texas, home of astronauts and the Johnson Space Center, the first victim in what was to become a cluster of suicides was a nineteen-year-old high school dropout who shot himself in the head as he sat in his car. His close friend turned a gun on himself in his pickup truck six weeks later. About fourteen days after that, another friend of both boys was found hanged from the top of a stairway in his home.

The list began to grow, and it spread beyond the original

circle of friends. A fifteen-year-old girl shot herself two days after the third suicide. But that was not the end of the tragedies. Only three more days passed before a sixteen-year-old boy hanged himself in his garage, and five days after that, a high school freshman died of carbon monoxide poisoning. The suicides in Clear Lake City made headlines across the country.

In Omaha, a visitor to Bryan High School, on the outskirts of the city, might at first glance have thought he was witnessing an ordinary pep rally. Cheerleaders dressed in the gold and green school colors led the student body in cheers for their athletic teams. Few students or teachers were absent.

But this was no regular pep assembly. Most of the students were wearing paper hearts bearing the words *Choose Life*. They sang the current hit tune "We Are the World." When they reached the line "We're saving our own lives," many of the teenagers were in tears. This pep rally had been called to calm the student body after three classmates committed suicide in five days.

The Omaha youths who took their lives were only vaguely acquainted. To the casual observer, they were teenagers with no apparent problems. The sixteen-year-old girl, who died from an overdose of her mother's antidepressant, was described as a positive, dependable person. Only very close friends knew she had faced serious problems with her boyfriend and had talked about dropping out of school.

The youngest of the three victims, a fifteen-year-old boy, was a popular and outgoing athlete who recently had spent a lot of time alone building a drill press. Because of this new interest, nobody thought his withdrawal from friends strange until they learned he had fatally shot himself in the chest.

The third victim was a young man of eighteen. Students described him as a loner and said he talked of going to a trade school once he was graduated from Bryan High School. According to police, he told a friend shortly before his death that he was disgusted with life.

Copycat suicides? A chain reaction? Coincidence? Whatever the answer, the cluster of self-destruction sent shock waves through the school. Counselors reported that some students dreaded going to class each day, fearing that another classmate would be dead. The question of who would be next hung in the minds of many students.

The two teenagers who committed suicide in North Salem, New York, knew each other well. The seventeen-year-old boy hanged himself just three weeks after his girlfriend had hanged herself. They had quarreled at a drive-in. Copycat? Coincidence?

In the spring of 1988, officials of the Fairview, Pennsylvania, high school canceled final exams and graduation for the senior class. They believed they had evidence of a suicide pact among friends of a senior who had fatally shot himself at Christmastime. According to rumor, a suicide would take place during the graduation ceremony.

No matter what circumstances surround the cluster suicides, some mental-health experts believe that urban living and community stress may play a role in the incidence of these deaths. Counselors in Plano, Texas, where eight students took their lives, noted that the city had undergone such rapid growth that few families had time to put down roots. Plano is an affluent community with high levels of divorce, many single parents, and dual-career families. All of these factors are frequently found in the backgrounds of young suicide victims.

However, the phenomenon of clustering is not confined to urban areas. Cheyenne, Wyoming, has a population of less than 50,000; yet it lost three young people to suicide in one month.

When three teenagers in Storm Lake, Iowa—population under 9,000—took their lives, it shook not only the community but the whole state. Some weeks after the deaths, psychologist Rita Frevert told a reporter it would cause a panic if residents of the town knew how many local young people she had seen during the year who had tried to kill themselves.

The truth remains that researchers know very little about cluster suicides. Several deaths falling in a relatively short time span may be coincidence. There is also the chance that a follow-up death may be a youth's self-dramatizing effort to capture the same outpouring of sympathy and attention that surrounded an earlier death.

Problems sometimes seem insurmountable to people in their teen and young adult years. When a classmate kills himself, other troubled students take heed. Suddenly suicide may seem like a reasonable way to deal with overwhelming troubles. It's almost as if a taboo has been lifted and the taking of one's life is now an acceptable act. A young person may be thinking, Hey, he did it and look at all the attention it got. People really felt badly, so why don't I do it too? On the other hand, if the dead person was a close friend, the survivor may identify so strongly with the victim that he may feel that he owes it to his friend to join him in death. This can be painfully true if he hears parents, teachers, and classmates talk of the suicide as foolish, crazy, or stupid. And it can also be true when he sees others going on about their daily lives, seeming to forget quickly the suicide victim and his pain.

A surviving friend may become furious at the indifference of others. He sees that his buddy, although he has sacrificed all, has really achieved nothing by his suicidal act. He has not gained the immortality he must have sought. And so, in the survivor's mind, it may become increasingly important to try to make his friend's death count by adding his own to it.

Many young people go through a normal period of depression and mourning for the loss of childhood attachments. Psychologists think that some boys kill themselves after breaking up with a girlfriend because they feel that the severed relationship points up their failure to leave the family orbit. When a young person's thinking becomes muddled with grief, anger, hopelessness, and depression, it is hard for him to see the many alternatives to taking his life. It is hard for him to explore other lifesaving options that can lessen his pain. But these alternatives and options exist, and it is up to friends and family to make the potential suicide victim aware of them.

Is suicide contagious? Does it tend to spread from person to person?

Facts suggest that the answer is yes.

There is no vaccine. There is no quick fix. But mental-health workers offer hope that positive steps can be taken to prevent suicide. Many communities that have been forced to deal with this problem have formulated preventive measures.

Survivors in these stricken communities express the hope that somewhere in the seemingly pointless deaths there is a lesson that will prevent future occurrences of the phenomenon. They feel that suicide is the ultimate form of communication and that these dead-and-gone-forever teenagers have left a strong message: They needed help they didn't receive.

6

The Warning Signs

It was past midnight on an August evening when sixteen-year-old Chad rushed home from a drinking party, ran to his room—passing his parents, who were waiting up for him—and ended his life with a shotgun blast. If he had given out any warning signs of this impending action, his parents had missed them.

Dan, a brilliant but troubled fifteen-year-old, came downstairs wearing a favorite baseball cap and carrying a suitcase of clothing. Although his parents were having him committed to a mental institution, he acted calm and collected. He hesitated a moment at the front door, then said he had to go to the bathroom. His parents waited, and when Dan reappeared, the family left the house together. But before they reached the car, Dan was vomiting. During those few moments in the bathroom he had taken poison—he died the next day.

Eleven-year-old Brian's essay was due on a Tuesday morning, and he turned it in on time, but it wasn't until Tuesday night that his teacher got around to grading the day's papers. Her concern grew as she read Brian's account of an eleven-year-old boy using a plastic bag to suffocate himself.

She immediately called the elementary school principal, and they agreed to seek counseling for Brian the next day. They were too late. Even as they were talking, paramedics were trying in vain to revive Brian, whose mother had found his body with a plastic bag pulled over his head.

Not all potential suicide victims may give out as deliberate a warning signal as Brian did, but most of the young people who take their own lives have shown one or more signs of their serious intention beforehand. This was true of the three boys just mentioned.

Chad's parents described him as a very methodical person. His father said that Chad's taking of his own life was the only snap decision he ever made. Usually, after returning home for the evening, Chad would go to his room and change his clothes, then spend time talking with his parents. They were a close family.

Teachers at Chad's school described him as the typical boy next door. He was a good student. He was popular with his peers. He worked part-time sacking groceries at a supermarket, and he loved sports. None of them considered him a candidate for suicide.

Friends drew a slightly different picture of Chad. He was well liked, but they described him as being confused and depressed. The night of his death he had talked to them of killing himself. Yes, he had been drinking, but not much. The county medical examiner stated that an autopsy report showed no sign of alcohol. Chad's friends said they joked with him, trying to shake him from his morbid mood. None of them had taken his suicide threats seriously.

Chad had given out warning signals, but everyone had missed or ignored them.

Dan had known nothing of the warm family life that Chad had experienced. When Dan was a week old, his father hanged himself in his jail cell. A year before Dan's death, his mother had remarried, and because of her son's antisocial behavior, she and his new stepfather sought counseling for him. His psychologist advised them to watch Dan closely and to act quickly should signs of violence occur. The parents feared as much for their own lives as for their son's.

Dan and Chad were nothing alike in personality. Dan's teachers described him as a troubled genius. A loner, he had experienced brushes with the law and with school officials, who suspected him of vandalism. He was highly intelligent, a child who had begun reading at age two and who, as a high school student, was attending some college classes. His favorite composers were Mozart and Beethoven, and he often stayed up all night listening to classical music.

His life reached the breaking point on the morning his mother refused him the use of her car. He walked to school in an angry huff, and that afternoon after classes, he locked himself in the basement of his home, where he turned off the water and the electricity. He also disconnected the TV cable. His parents, fearing violence, called a friend to stay in the house with him while they made legal arrangements to have him committed to a mental institution. As it turned out, their help came too late.

Sixth-grader Brian had given warning signals of his impending death even before he wrote the essay that alerted his teacher and the school principal. He and his family had recently moved to their present home, and Brian had been seeing a counselor at the county mental-health center because he had had difficulty adjusting to his new school and his new classmates.

His parents had not thought of Brian as suicidal. They considered his problems with his classmates minor, and they and his counselor had thought they were getting positive results. Even his teachers had remarked that there was a change for the better in Brian's attitude.

Brian's case again points up the fact that many times parents, teachers, and counselors know less about a person than that person's peer group. After Brian's death, classmates who had known him reported that he had mentioned that he was considering suicide. They thought he was joking, but he was definitely sending out signals that were ignored.

Many self-inflicted deaths might be prevented if people were trained to recognize the warning signals. Mental-health specialists estimate that all potential suicides give at least one warning, and that 80 percent of them give repeated warnings. As is true in many cases, hindsight is sometimes twenty-twenty vision, while foresight is murky and muddled.

There are many signs that set the stage for a future suicide. Some troubled people show their life-taking intent through their behavior. They may give away prized possessions. It's not uncommon for a troubled child or young adult to give away his record collection, his baseball cards, even favorite pieces of clothing. The recipient of such a gift should immediately be on the alert and take steps to get help for his friend.

Noticeable changes in eating habits can be a signal of trouble ahead. The stressed person may either stop eating or he may dramatically increase his food intake. One situation is as dangerous as the other. Such actions are calls for help.

The Warning Signs

Changes in sleeping habits should also be considered warning signals. Listen to the person who tells you he can't sleep. Listen to the person who seems to be trying to hide from the world by sleeping all the time. Both these people may be subtly saying that they intend to take their lives.

If a person suddenly withdraws from family, friends, or his regular activities and seems bored with everything, his behavior and actions should be scrutinized. All people experience periods of boredom at different times in their lives, but when that life-style becomes persistent, it could be a sign of depression and trouble ahead.

A decline in the quality of schoolwork should be a clue to parents, teachers, and peers that a person may be deeply troubled. The good or average student who is thinking of taking his life may suddenly seem to have difficulty in concentrating, and he may seem to care nothing about his classes or his grades.

Suicide warning signals also come in the form of violent or rebellious behavior. Such actions are especially significant when they appear in a person who has previously been docile and easy to get along with.

"When a lady from Casey's convenience store called me and said, 'Honey, your kids are down here trying to buy sleeping pills,' I knew something was wrong." This statement came from a Midwestern foster mother of five children ranging in ages from four to twelve. The children had been taken away from their mentally disturbed mother amid allegations of child abuse, and they had been placed in a foster home. When the court initiated action to return the children to their mother, the children rebelled.

The older two pooled their allowance money to buy sleeping pills. This was a joint decision, and they told the store clerk that their mother was having trouble sleeping. Later the oldest child told her foster mother that the court would never get her alive. She said if they took her away from the only love and happiness she'd ever known, she might as well not live.

In this case, which drew national headlines, warning signs were heeded, and the children's lives were saved.

The young person who runs away from home has designed his behavior to deliver a message. He's asking for help at the same time that he seems to be trying to distance himself from those who can give that help. Troubled young people may be unable to communicate with their parents, so they run away. They may have developed problems at school or on the job, and these factors may work together to generate drug or alcohol use. Or the substance use may come first. It may lead to problems at home and at school. Unfortunately, substance use aggravates the person's problems and may increase his depression and his suicidal tendencies.

Young people who are suicidal may also develop physical complaints such as stomachache, headache, or general feelings of chronic fatigue. These complaints are warning signals.

A potential suicide may use body language to send out his plea for help. Such warning signs are easy to miss, but they can be spotted by the careful observer who knows what he's looking for.

One therapist reported that his last patient of the day, a seventeen-year-old boy, sat listlessly in the office with his arms crossed and his eyes vague. He was slumped over and passive. When the boy told the therapist that he wasn't going to worry about tomorrow, that there wouldn't be any tomorrow for him, the therapist took it calmly at first.

This boy had threatened suicide every week for the past six months, but he hadn't followed through with action.

Yet, as he closed his office for the day, the doctor became uneasy about this patient. A worrisome message had come across during the counseling session. The empty face, the listless posture, the crossed arms—all were spelling out a message in body language. The boy was telling the therapist what he meant to do. Words had become useless to him. In the past he had tried crying out, but to no avail. Now his body was speaking for him.

Luckily, the therapist followed his hunch that his patient meant business this time. He closed his office and drove to the boy's house. He alerted the youth's parents to the situation, and they found that the boy had taken a bottle of pills from the medicine cabinet and swallowed them behind the locked door of his bedroom. An emetic cleaned the boy's stomach in time to save his life.

Behavior and body language can help identify a potential suicide, but some of the most important signals are verbal. As was the case with Chad and Brian, spoken warnings may be taken as jokes and ignored. Such comments should never be passed over lightly.

The troubled person may make statements such as "I wish I'd never been born," or "You're going to be sorry when I'm gone," or "I want to go to sleep and never wake up." He might also say "Nothing matters anymore," or "I won't be a problem for you much longer." Remarks such as these should be taken as seriously as if the person had said "I'm going to kill myself."

Sometimes people who have given off some of these warning signals suddenly seem to do a turnaround. After a period of seeming bored or depressed, they all at once become pleasant and cheerful. Their friends may be happy to think the person is at last on the way to recovery, but this may not be the case. It is quite possible that the troubled person is suddenly cheerful because he has pulled himself from the gloom of indecision by definitely deciding to take his life. This decision has relieved him of much stress, and this relief is the basis of his seeming change for the better.

The warning signals a potential suicide may be sending out can be many and varied. A well-adjusted person may also be sending out some of the same signals. Not all people who lose their appetites are suicidal. Not all people who suddenly lack interest in school are thinking of ending their lives. But when a life may be at stake, it is unwise to ignore such warnings. It is far better to heed a false signal and be mistaken, and perhaps laughed at, than it is to ignore that signal and then feel sorrow and guilt at a suicide victim's funeral.

You can help prevent suicide by listening and by taking action.

7

One Girl's Story

> Trapped in a battlefield.
> No door to escape through.
> Where am I to go?
> Where am I to run to?
> No one on my side.
> No one believes
> That inside this mean,
> All-her-fault girl
> Is an over-her-age child
> Screaming.

Seventeen-year-old Michelle Jones from south Florida wrote these opening lines to a much longer poem when she was twelve. Now, five years later, after an unsuccessful suicide attempt, she is no longer running. She is no longer seeking escape. Instead, she is self-supporting and living in a rented trailer home in a quiet neighborhood in the Florida Keys. Most important of all, she has regained her self-respect, and she no longer thinks of suicide as her only way out.

Michelle attempted to take her life when she was sixteen. When asked if it had been a spur-of-the-moment decision, she replied that in a way it had, but that in many ways it hadn't. A bitter fight with her boyfriend precipitated the actions that might have caused her death.

"It was a terrible fight. It left me feeling like a total failure. Everything came to a head. I realized that I couldn't get along with my mother, I couldn't get along with the kids and the teachers at school, and now I couldn't get along with my boyfriend. I felt hopeless and defeated. I saw death as my only way out."

Michelle's attempt to take her life was not carefully planned. She left no suicide note because she was too upset over the fight with her boyfriend to think about writing. Her thoughts were on finding a quick way to kill herself. She found a handgun that her mother kept in their home for protection, and she considered using it to shoot herself. Then she reconsidered. She knew nothing about guns. What would happen if her aim was poor? What if the bullet missed a vital spot and she only injured herself? She was afraid she couldn't stand the pain and suffering that might be involved in a nonfatal shooting. Her thoughts raced. Knives, too, were out of the question. Too much blood. Too great a chance for prolonged pain.

Then she went to the family medicine cabinet. Her mother had kept unused prescription drugs following surgery the previous year, so Michelle decided to swallow pills as an easy way out. She imagined that such a death would be similar to going to sleep. She held the pill bottle in her hand, having no idea what this medication was, or how much of it would be required to induce death. She just swallowed what she hoped would be a lethal dose.

"I didn't expect anyone to appear and rescue me," Michelle said. "I knew my mother was out with her boyfriend for the evening, and I thought I'd be dead long before she returned home. I sat around in the living room for a while, waiting for the pills to take effect, but nothing happened. Then I decided to go out and walk until I felt the pills taking hold. I walked for a long time, and when I began to feel drowsy, I went home. I lay down on the living room couch, expecting to pass out and die; but before this happened, my mother and her friend returned home and found me.

"I went berserk. I was so angry to have failed—again. It took the two of them to hold me down until I became more calm. Mother found the gun where I had tossed it on a bed, and she guessed from that that something was really wrong. Then she noticed the raided medicine chest and the scattered pill bottles.

"She remembered about how many pills she had taken, and she counted the remaining pills, many of which were antibiotics. Then she called the doctor. He told her I hadn't taken enough of the drugs to kill me, and he said to put me to bed and let me sleep it off.

"I slept for a day and a half. When I woke up, it was as if the attempt hadn't happened. I could hardly remember it. I probably wanted to forget it. I was very glad I was still alive, but I was really mad at myself. I'd always thought of myself as a very strong person. I *hated* knowing I'd been weak enough to let life get me so down I'd try a dumb thing like suicide."

When Michelle said that in many ways her suicide attempt was *not* a spur-of-the-moment decision, she was thinking of the problems that had beset her since she was a preschooler. She is the youngest of three sisters. Her parents fought, sometimes violently, until they were divorced. Michelle's father dropped out of her life when she was five years old. Many times during her early years, family members had told her that she had been her father's favorite child, his princess. She enjoyed hearing this, and she created a fantasy world in which she was her father's darling.

The divorce was hard on both Michelle and her family. Her mother, refusing welfare assistance, went to work at entry-level wages to support herself and her three daughters. She held down two jobs, literally working day and night. There was no money for baby-sitters. At night, Michelle was left in the supervision of a teenage sister nine years her senior.

Sometimes this arrangement worked out well, but many times the older sister wanted to go out with her boyfriend. She resented being tied down to younger siblings. To buy her own freedom for a few hours, she would give Michelle and her other sister money and tell them to go somewhere.

Michelle recalls that many nights when she was around nine and ten years old, she roamed the streets of Miami until midnight, returning home just before her mother came in from her late-night job. None of the three sisters told their mother what was going on at home while she was working.

When Michelle's father reappeared in her life, she was twelve. He paid no special attention to her and gave no indication that she was his favorite child. The dream she had built up around him shattered; Michelle felt betrayed and unloved. She was a pretty, well-developed girl, and in her need for a father figure and male approval, she became involved with a boyfriend five years older than she was.

At this time, she also became truant at school, and she

was a discipline problem both at home and in the classroom. Michelle admitted that she refused to listen to her mother, or her school counselors. She felt that nobody understood her.

"All those counselors knew was what they had read in books. They said they knew what I was going through, but they didn't. They couldn't know. They had never been in a situation like mine, so there was no way they could really understand anything about the pain I was feeling.

"I've had lots of counselors. Once I had ten different ones in a two-year period. It really wasn't their fault that they couldn't help me. They were overworked. Sometimes one counselor would be trying to help a hundred people. Nobody can handle a case load like that. One woman did help me—a little. She made me realize that to succeed I must care about myself and look for my good points. I've always remembered that."

When her mother realized she could no longer cope with Michelle, she asked that this daughter be declared a ward of the court, hoping she would receive the help she needed. Michelle spent four months in a hospital for the emotionally disturbed before moving to a state-sponsored youth home.

"I also did time in a residence hall that offered help to people with family problems," Michelle said, her choice of words indicating that the hall was more of a prison than a home.

Now and then during those troubled years, the court returned Michelle to her mother's custody on a trial basis. Michelle seized the opportunity to run away during one of those visits home, and she was gone for several weeks.

"I want you to know that I was never a prostitute. Lots

of runaways turn to prostitution in order to exist. I didn't do that. I lived in an apartment in Miami. Sometimes I had to steal in order to pay the bills.

"Eventually I started supporting myself by selling cocaine. A boyfriend gave me the cocaine, and I sold it on Freak's Corner outside my school. I took my cut of the money and passed the rest on to him.

"Nobody tried to stop me. The teachers? They were glad to have me out of their classrooms and out of their hair. They knew pushers were dealing drugs right outside the school, but they turned their backs. If they had tried to do anything to prevent it, it would have meant a lot of grief for them—catching me in the act, hiring lawyers to prosecute, going to court. They didn't want the hassle.

"I wasn't aware of it, but while I was away from home, my mother and the police were frantically looking for me. They didn't find me. I finally got tired of the runaway life and went back home. My family was glad to see me, and we tried to work out our differences.

"During my time as a runaway, I didn't use the drugs I was pushing, but after I returned home, I began using cocaine. I enjoyed the highs, but I really hated the coming down. Cocaine was ruining my looks. I was pale and drawn, and my hair looked terrible. I had always been proud of my appearance. So when friends started telling me I looked like hell, I stopped using cocaine. Just like that. I don't think I'm an addictive person. I stopped without any problem. Lots of kids who get started can't stop. That's a real danger.

"My mother managed to get a college degree, and she got a job in real estate that allowed her to be home much more than she had been in the past. She decided I would be better off away from Miami and in a smaller school, so we moved to the Keys. This didn't work out for me. It was hard to go from a high school of several thousand to one of several hundred.

"In Miami, my actions were sometimes lost in the crowd, but in the Keys, in a small school, everyone noticed me and they noticed everything I did that was out of line. I was suspended eighteen times for various offenses before I finally dropped out in my junior year. It was during this time that I swallowed the pills.

"My mother complains that I choose the wrong kind of friends, the druggies, the lowlifes, the losers. She may be right, but as long as I can see one good thing about a person, I'll be that person's friend. I know how it is to be down and out and to have nobody believe in you."

From this account, one might think that life holds little promise for Michelle, but she has taken some very positive steps. She feels certain there will be no more suicide attempts. She doesn't blame her mother for any of her past problems, realizing that her mother was all but overwhelmed trying to support the family and earn a college degree—a degree that would help her advance to better-paying employment and the chance to spend more time with her children.

Michelle does say that she has some questions she wants to ask her father. Up until this time she has only heard her mother's side of the story, and Michelle believes that in all fairness she needs to hear her father's side too before she makes any lasting judgments about him and about her relationship to him.

"I've taken my General Educational Development test to earn a high school diploma, and I think I'll pass. I've always made straight A's when I've worked at it. I'm smart and I've got a good brain. When I get my diploma, I plan to enroll in college in Miami. I want to be a counselor and help other kids, not because counselors helped me a lot, but because kids in trouble need to talk to someone who's really been there, someone who knows firsthand what it's like to have gone through all the things I've been through. I think I can help others who face the same problems I've faced, and I'd like to do that."

And so, while she waits for news of that diploma, Michelle is working for a local business as she lives with a friend in her neat and clean trailer home with a pit bull puppy for protection.

8

One Boy's Story

Whenever a young person kills himself, there is speculation about his motive. Even if the youth leaves a note, it may not totally explain the reasons for his despair.

It is impossible to interview a suicide victim, but Sam Smith (a pseudonym), whose heart stopped beating three times and who lay in a coma for days following his attempt to take his life, agreed to tell his story. He hopes to encourage troubled youths to seek better ways of solving their problems.

At the time of his attempt, Sam was a high school senior, living on a small farm in Ohio with his parents, a twin brother, and a younger sister. Both of Sam's parents have successful careers, and as a family project, the Smiths raise a few head of livestock. The family is highly regarded in their community, and for years they have supported church, school, and civic affairs.

When people heard about Sam's suicide attempt, they asked, "Why would a bright kid like Sam do this? He's popular. He's brilliant. He's got everything in the world going for him. But he's impulsive and he's got a temper.

Maybe that explains it." People couldn't have guessed farther from the truth.

When asked if his suicide attempt was a spur-of-the-moment decision, Sam smiled and shook his head.

"Hardly. I remember sitting in a third-grade classroom, staring out the window and wondering why my dad didn't love me. I wondered what I could do to make him like me better. I really wanted to please him.

"I grew up without feeling enough affection in my home. It wasn't a place where love was freely given, and I grew up as many kids do. I wasn't alone, but I thought I was. This doesn't mean that my parents didn't care for me. I know now that they did and that they still do. It's just that a lot of their ways were ways they learned from their own parents. Raising kids isn't an exact science, but kids need unconditional love from somewhere, and where can they get it in this society?

"At home I felt I didn't get enough attention and affection from my parents. On the school playground I didn't get along with the kids, partly because I was an egghead and partly because I wasn't well coordinated and didn't excel in sports.

"However, in elementary school I did realize I was smart, and I started to use my intellect to earn affection. I soon learned that scholars got favorable attention and that they were considered good kids. So I became a 'good' boy. In elementary school, I was easy to get along with. The teachers liked me—probably because by applying my ability to learn, I made them feel successful.

"At the time I didn't realize why I was making this all-out bid for approval. The things I'm telling you are my thoughts now in looking back on those times. Kids pick on one another in grade school, and I was picked on. It hurt. Having teacher approval lessened the hurt.

"So eventually, I left this rural school and entered junior high in a nearby city. There I tried to become a perfectionist. The more perfect I became, I thought, the more attention I would get from everyone.

"I got to the point where small errors were a big, big deal. If I made one little mistake, my image of myself was shattered. If I played a wrong note in band, I'd think about it for the next ten measures and mess up the whole piece. I was going to compete for attention by being perfect. The plan worked fairly well until I got to high school.

"There, it became clear to me that everything isn't perfect and that I couldn't make it perfect no matter how determined I might be. I began to realize that life isn't an easy thing.

"I excelled in many areas. I had a four-point average, but I wasn't the best. I started realizing that there were people better than me. Maybe a lot of them.

"Everything was beginning to come to a head. Life was becoming more difficult. I felt terrible and everything seemed hopeless. People ask me now why I didn't talk my problems over with someone. That's hard to do.

"I didn't tell my parents how I felt. I didn't feel close enough to friends to tell them how I was feeling. My twin brother? I didn't talk to him either. Twins want to develop individual personalities. I felt my brother was pushing me away in order to create his own identity. I didn't feel as much of a need to be rid of him.

"I talked to no one about my feelings. I thought people wouldn't listen, or if they did listen, that they'd tell me I shouldn't feel the way I felt. School counselor? No. Minister? No—too remote.

"I lived in the country, and that made it kind of hard to mingle with friends. Then my brother started wanting to do his own thing. He was good at getting along with other kids. I felt that life just wasn't working out for me. I didn't have much communication with anyone.

"I was scared to death that all my friends were going to leave me. In my senior year, I got to the point of asking myself, Where's the love? I don't see any love around here anywhere. According to society, the ultimate love is between a male and a female, so I got into a relationship with a girl. This was my last-ditch effort to find love and affection.

"A lot of people think a guy commits suicide because his girl jilted him, when in reality the relationship with the girl was his last-ditch effort to find love—and it failed. This is what happened to me. When my girlfriend turned me away, I saw myself as a failure and I decided to end it all.

"I couldn't get it together with my parents. I couldn't get it together with my friends. And now I couldn't get it together with this girl. I stood in front of the kitchen window. I had thought of committing suicide for a month ahead of this time. I had written a letter and torn it up. People who commit suicide don't really want to die. They want to live.

"But I didn't see any love around me. I've gone to church all of my life. I'd heard there's a loving God, so I decided to go where He is. I had taken some stuff from the high school chemistry lab—a clear crystal that would easily dissolve in liquid. I didn't have suicide in mind when I stole this stuff. We keep livestock, and some of the critters can be stubborn. The substance I took from school is sometimes used in hypnosis. My original idea was to slip a little to the critters when they became balky. I had read about the substance, and I knew that it could be fatal if taken in large amounts. I swallowed a lot of it. I never doubted that it would do the job.

"Almost immediately I had misgivings, but I didn't know what to do. I probably wasn't thinking clearly at that time. The solution was already beginning to take effect. The last thing I remember was walking upstairs to my room.

"I woke up in a hospital, angry and grumbling. I was still alive. My plan had failed. What was I going to do now? Later I learned that my brother found me on the floor. When he and my mother couldn't rouse me, she called an ambulance to get me to the hospital. I almost died. I also learned that one of my junior high teachers had spent the three days I was comatose near my hospital bed praying for me. It touched me deeply to know that he cared about me that much.

"Then people started visiting. My grandpa. My family. I didn't know what I was thinking most of the time. I remembered the attempt, but my mind was muddled. The mother of a friend visited me, telling me that once she had tried to take her life, and that the first thing I had to do was to forgive myself. Then her daughter came in and said, 'Sam, I want you to know we all forgive you.' That hit me, because I didn't know I needed to be forgiven. I started realizing that these people felt betrayed. It had already struck them that life isn't all a breeze. They felt as if I had given up, and it made them angry.

"I was moved from the hospital to a mental-health unit, and doctors ordered medication for depression. This was the first time I'd heard of depression or heard that it was a type of mental illness. And I still had it. I felt awful. I'd be walking down the ward halls, and I wouldn't even see the walls, I was so down. I didn't think I'd ever be able to do anything pleasant or enjoyable again.

"Then more friends started visiting. They'd never talk about my suicide attempt. It was the healthiest thing they could have done. These kids gave me encouragement by taking time just to be with me, and we always had something to do. We talked. We played games. We watched TV. Their being there said, 'Hey, we accept you and we appreciate you and we're taking time to come see you.' I needed this because I felt so worthless.

"In this mental ward, one special doctor would stop to talk to me about calculus. He was like a friend. I thought I was socially inept, but he'd pause at my doorway and take time from his rounds to talk with me. We'd work calculus problems. I'd do the problem, and at first I'd want to jump right in and tell him how I'd done it. Gradually I learned to wait and let him think about it, solve it himself; then we'd discuss the solution together. This reassured me that I did have some social skills.

"One day a friend came to visit. In leaving, he reached toward me, and I gripped his arm with my left hand. As I did this, I felt a kind of slow electricity go through me. It was so comforting. It's hard for me to explain now, but I thought, What is this? The answer eluded me.

"I thought a lot about that hospital. People were running it. Humans. They weren't perfect, yet the place really ran and did good things for people. I wondered at the power that held it together. Some of the nurses had gone through divorce. Some had seen their children die. Their problems appeared a lot deeper than mine. I wondered what gave them the strength to go on.

"I remembered how caring my doctor was, and I

thought, I want to be like that. I want to be a doctor and help people. I really felt a warm glow similar to the one I had felt earlier when I had gripped my friend's arm. That moment left me with the knowledge that someone with a power greater than I could imagine loved me and was going to stay with me through all of this. I felt surrounded by love, and somehow I knew it would be there always.

"After that, I learned and grew by spending time with my friends. Relationships were important to me. I saw a mental-health specialist two times a week. Then I got back into school. I dropped one class. One English teacher gave me an A, and it encouraged me. I decided to go out for track. I had never done that before. I didn't train properly for it and I was discouraged with the results, but my coaches would listen to me, and they encouraged me to stay with it. They were the first people to teach me not to have over-expectations for myself.

"*Don't should on me.* Those words became my motto. The word *should* can hold you in bondage. Of course, there are times and circumstances when I need to say *should,* but now I go easy with that word.

"I went on to an Ivy League college and did fine the first year. Now, in my second year, I've dropped out to work for a while, to try to gain the financial independence that will let me have more control of my life. I intend to enroll in college again, and I have some scholarship money to help with expenses.

"From this whole experience I'm learning that human love is a give-and-take sort of thing. I give. I expect to receive. I can only give so much; then I need to have something pumped back into me in return. But in addition to human love, I've now become aware of God's ever-present love all around me, and I can be completely filled with it. In accordance with this universal spirit of love, I receive by giving. I give and expect nothing in return. It makes me stop expecting love from people and thus hating them and feeling angry when I don't get it.

"I have learned to recognize a loving presence in the universe and beautiful things in nature. These are a blessing to me. I no longer feel a need to go where a loving God is. He is all around me. Anyone thinking about committing suicide is really looking for life. That person really wants to live, whether or not he recognizes that fact. I'm glad to be here."

9

How to Help Your Friend

He always wanted to explain things.
But no one cared.
So he drew.
Sometimes he would draw, and it wasn't anything.
He wanted to carve it in stone
or write it in the sky,
and it would be only him and the sky
and the things inside him that needed saying.
It was after that he drew the picture.
He drew all yellow.
It was the way he felt about morning,
and it was beautiful.
The teacher smiled at him.
"What's this?" she said, "Why don't you
draw something like Ken's drawing?
Isn't that beautiful?"
After that, his mother bought him a tie,
and he always drew airplanes and rocketships
like everyone else.
And he threw the old picture away.

> And when he lay alone looking at the sky,
> it was big and blue and all of everything,
> but he wasn't anymore.
> He was square inside and brown,
> and his hands were stiff.
> He was like everyone else.
> The things inside that needed saying
> didn't need it anymore.
> It had stopped pushing.
> It was crushed.
> Stiff.
> Like everything else.

This poem appeared on the front page of an Iowa high school newspaper. Written by a senior just two weeks before he killed himself, the poem reflects the hopeless feelings that suicide victims often feel. His suicide left an aftermath of shock among the student body.

When a young person takes his life, shock waves are felt throughout his school and community. Friends begin soul-searching, asking themselves if they should have known this classmate was suicidal and wondering if they could have done anything to prevent his death.

In addition to the loss of a valuable life, another very damaging effect of suicide is the guilt felt by so many of the people who knew the victim. In retrospect, they realize that they missed, misinterpreted, or ignored the troubled person's warning signals. They feel that they might have been able to do something to help. They may be wondering how they can deal with their guilt, and they may be very angry with the deceased for putting them in this position. They also may think they are very much alone with these uncomfortable thoughts and the hurt they bring.

It may help these people to remember that uppermost in the mind of the suicidal person is the desire to end his own emotional pain, not to add to the pain of others. Just about everyone who has lost someone to suicide wonders if he could have done something to prevent the tragedy.

These survivors need to realize that hindsight is better than foresight. Those who are left behind shouldn't blame themselves for things they didn't understand at a time when they might have helped, had they been more knowledgeable. The suicide might have taken place in spite of their best efforts to prevent it.

You may be thinking that you don't know any classmates or acquaintances who feel suicidal, but this may not be true. Take a careful look at your friends; then ask yourself a few thoughtful questions.

Why does Tim do drugs and act so rebelliously? Why do Dan and Barry drag race through the streets at night? Where has Jenny been lately? Why has Carol lost so much weight? Why is Hank suddenly keeping to himself?

And don't forget to give some careful consideration to your cheerleader friend who earns straight A's and who has had a date every Friday night for the past two years. Her appearance of success may be only a façade. One small failure could shatter her self-image and plunge her into despair.

Suicide is the most preventable cause of death. Mental-health specialists believe that the majority of teenage suicides can be prevented if people close to the troubled ones heed the warning signs and step in to give assistance. Statistics show that many troubled young people turn first to their friends for help because they feel that friends will be less controlling and more objective than parents or teachers. It is important that you be there for such people. By being there, you may be able to save a life.

What can you do? You want to help. But how?

When you suspect that a friend is depressed and may be on the verge of suicide, you may feel anxious. You may feel embarrassed. But most likely of all, you may feel afraid. It is a scary situation. Throughout your life you may frequently use your peers as mirrors to help you evaluate your own progress and accomplishments. Friends who are well and happy reflect a positive image that gives you confidence, but you may feel threatened when a friend with serious problems reflects a troubled image. In your mind, you may be thinking, If it can happen to him, it can happen to me.

Before you can help a friend in trouble, you must overcome your own fears and move beyond them. This requires emotional courage. Such courage can be developed when you understand both the seriousness of the problem and the various ways of dealing with it. Suicidal people believe they cannot be helped, but the truth is, they can. With time, most of them can be restored to a full and happy life. They don't realize this; when they are feeling hopeless, their judgment is impaired. If you detect in your friend any of the warning signals mentioned in this book, it is time for you to help. Your friend needs you.

Begin by talking. Let your troubled friend know you care enough about him to discuss his problems with him. Let him know you know he's hurting and that you would like to help. You needn't worry that talking about suicide will put the idea into your friend's head. If he's feeling deeply troubled and depressed, thoughts of death are already there. Bringing them into the open can be helpful.

It is usually best to avoid asking point-blank if your friend is thinking of taking his life. Such a question may only result in a denial, and it may increase his guilt feelings. Instead, you might ask if he is feeling very unhappy. If he says yes, you could comment that sometimes unhappiness can make a person feel that life isn't worthwhile. It may help to share your own feelings about times when you've felt depressed.

Then you can ease more deeply into the subject by commenting that it's not uncommon for thoughts of suicide to cross the mind of anyone who is depressed. You may suggest that your friend has had such thoughts. If he has, he will usually admit it, and in most cases, he will feel a sense of relief and a lessening of the guilt feelings that have been building up inside him.

Follow talking with listening. It's often tempting to jump from problem to possible solution too quickly. Resist this temptation. Let your friend vent his feelings. He is under stress, and the stress process has three parts. There are the factors causing the stress, the increased negative feelings, and finally the action taken. By letting the troubled person express his feelings, you have a better chance of influencing him to take a positive action rather than a negative one.

Once your friend has admitted that thoughts of suicide have crossed his mind, pay careful attention to whatever he has to say. Listen closely. Accept his comments and take them seriously. Don't say things like "Snap out of it; you're being silly" or "That's ridiculous. Everything will be okay." He would have snapped out of it long ago if it had been within his power to do so. From his viewpoint, he's not being silly or ridiculous, and he feels certain that everything is not going to be okay. It's the seeming hopelessness of his situation that is getting to him.

It is also unwise to add to his guilt by reminding him how awful his parents and friends would feel if he killed himself. Nor does it help to mention that he has everything to live for and that he shouldn't feel the way he feels. Never debate whether suicide is right or wrong. This may only serve to make the person feel even more guilty and worthless.

Instead of making judgmental responses as you listen, tell your friend that you understand how disappointments can wound. Empathizing with his hurt can diminish the intensity of his emotional pain. However, if you show too much empathy, your comments may reinforce your friend's reasons for considering suicide by encouraging him to believe that everything in his life really is terrible beyond endurance.

Keep your remarks neutral. You might say "I'm worried about you and I want to help you," or "I understand." If you say something like "I know you're feeling so awful you don't want to live anymore," your nonjudgmental words may defuse a crisis and enable the person to consider the many other options and more rational solutions that are open to him.

The effectiveness of this technique was demonstrated in a class of graduate students at a midwestern university. Following an important midterm test, some students were discussing their grades. One straight-A student, who was deeply disappointed to have received a B+, made serious threats to end his life.

"You're breaking my heart," joked a friend who felt thankful to have received a B− on his test.

"You've got to be crazy," retorted another friend, unaware that the potential victim was growing more angry and depressed by the moment. "B+. Big deal!"

A third friend, more aware of the significance of the conversation, spoke up, saying, "Hey, buddy, I know how it is. It hurts, doesn't it? It really hurts."

While the other students went on about their own affairs, these two remained behind to talk about the "bad" grade. The resulting conversation led the troubled student to realize that he had many options other than death. He elected to seek and receive professional therapy that helped him continue his studies and earn his degree.

Help your friend focus on his exact problem. After you've talked and listened and empathized with your friend's troubles and his feelings, it's time to try to steer his thoughts away from death. Studies of suicidal people have shown that many of them are poor problem solvers. They have trouble seeing into the heart of a difficulty and formulating reasonable and possible solutions. You can help by assisting in outlining what needs to be done or changed. You may also try to suggest resources that could help him make these desired changes.

If the current problem has been an ongoing one, remind your friend how he faced a similar situation and coped with it in the past. Remind him of his successes, and suggest that if he uses the same, or a slightly modified approach, he might be successful again. At the end of this discussion, get him to agree to do something constructive to change the circumstances that are troubling him, and try to get him to consent to report back to you on the outcome of these actions.

Point out the benefits of professional help. If your friend balks at seeing a school counselor, a religious adviser, or a professional therapist, urge him to keep in contact with you. Arrange with him to talk in person or by telephone again within the next few hours, and keep this communication channel open by ending each talk session with a definite plan and time for the next one.

Keep no secrets. A friend who is considering suicide may try to make you give a pledge of secrecy. Avoid doing this if you can. If you can't, then make the promise, knowing in your mind that you're going to break it. It would be both foolish and dangerous for you to be aware of a potential suicide without seeking aid. Your friend's parents or other responsible adults should be informed immediately, and they should get professional help for your friend at once. Your friend may hate you when he realizes you've revealed his secret, but, with luck, he will live to thank you later.

Since you have no intention of keeping your friend's situation a secret, avoid expecting him to make heavy promises to you. Don't ask him to give his word that he won't kill himself. Instead, ask him to call you if he feels the urge to take his life. Point out again that you care and that you would want to talk to him once more before he takes any final steps.

When you try to help a troubled person, you sometimes must make difficult decisions. Although you've probably had no professional training in dealing with a potential suicide, you can, through questioning, determine the seriousness of the situation. It is possible to learn just how close your friend is to actually taking his life. To make this determination, it is sometimes helpful to discuss suicide as a practical and impending act. If the plans he reveals are generalized and vague, there is probably ample time for more talk and to secure the help of a school counselor or therapist.

If, in reply to your queries about his plans, your friend gives you step-by-step details concerning how he is going to take his life, you can be sure his intent is deadly serious and that he may implement the plan soon.

Ask hard questions. This is the time to make specific inquiries of a very practical and personal nature. Exactly how is your friend going to carry out his suicidal plan? Is he sure he can do it successfully? What if he botches it up? Can he stand the embarrassment of such a failure? What if he doesn't die and ends up brain damaged or paralyzed? Who will find his body? Will the finder be a loved one who may be traumatized for life?

These are harsh questions, but they can be helpful. They can strip all romance and mystery from the idea of suicide and reveal it for what it is—a totally serious and irrevocable act. These queries will help force a troubled person to realize that taking his life is permanent and that there are other solutions to his problems.

Take action. If you think your friend is in immediate danger of suicide, have all lethal weapons such as guns, knives, razor blades, matches, pills, or drugs removed from his reach.

Never leave a person alone who is on the brink of taking his life. In his mental anguish, he may shout and scream, telling you to go away or ordering you to leave. Ignore his words. Don't be afraid of invading his privacy. Stay with him. Suicide records show that in almost every case, death would have been prevented had someone remained with the troubled person. Stay. This is another case in which your friend may hate you at the time but live to thank you later.

While you're staying with a person who is contemplating suicide, call the police if the situation seems immediately life threatening. This may be as simple as dialing 911 if you live in an area that recognizes this police emergency number, or dialing 0 for operator assistance if you do not. After the police have been called, you should contact a suicide-prevention center. Telephone numbers for these crisis centers are listed in the phone book under Suicide, Crisis, Mental Health, or Counseling.

If a situation is not of an emergency nature, a good way to find the closest crisis center is to call the American Association of Suicidology at 303-692-0985 during business hours. An AAS staff member will refer you to the nearest center. This group also publishes an updated directory of suicide-prevention centers, which is available for $10.00 by writing AAS, 2459 South Ash, Denver, Colorado 80222.

Talk. Listen. Focus on the exact problem. Point out the benefits of professional help. Keep no secrets. Ask hard questions. Take action.

These are some of the answers to questions about how you can help a friend. The sad truth is that many people who attempt suicide really don't want to die. In many cases, they just want a friend who cares. Be there. Your efforts may very well save a life.

10

How Schools Can Help

Although cluster suicides have shocked the nation, they also have served to create a determination within school systems to take steps in preventing future tragedies. The schools are taking action, but many teachers, counselors, and parents are concerned that students may be getting false messages from these actions. Does talking about suicide prevent tragedies? Or does it actually encourage youths to take their lives?

Some psychiatrists say schools are endangering lives when they teach pupils about suicide. They point out that studies of school antidrug programs in the 1970s showed that drug use went up, not down, after the drug education classes.

Advocates of school suicide education programs say the steady rise in adolescent suicide rates over the last three decades makes educating youngsters worth the risk. Charlotte Ross, suicidologist for the Youth Suicide National Center, feels that the continuing frequency of suicide among the nation's youth shows that avoiding the topic hasn't worked.

This issue is being put to the test in New Jersey, where a Columbia University team is conducting the first extensive research project in the nation on whether suicide education in school is part of the problem or part of the solution. The state of New Jersey has hired this team to study three pilot projects, including a suicide-prevention course in two Jersey City high schools that is almost identical to the one used in Bergenfield and other Bergen County schools.

One of these courses clearly identifies itself to students as oriented to suicide prevention. A second program focuses on coping with stress and developing problem-solving skills. The third project takes an even more indirect approach to the subject of suicide.

The New Jersey state legislature has spent $300,000 to fund the three pilot programs, the Columbia University team, and an advisory council to review all the results. Legislation is pending to appropriate another $78,000 to extend the project.

Attempting to discern whether talking about suicide in the classroom encourages suicide attempts, the Columbia team will check emergency room records for several weeks following the classes.

Teachers are a valuable resource in preventing suicide because they spend so much time with young people, and they frequently are aware of what a young person's life is really like. A teacher knows which student cuts classes, which student reports for school high on alcohol or stoned on drugs, or which child is suddenly depressed. He or she is aware of a student's dropping grades.

Dr. Mary Jane Rotheram of the Columbia University College of Physicians and Surgeons' Department of Child Psychiatry has devised a simple test to help teachers tell if a student is in imminent danger to himself. According to Dr.

Rotheram, evidence of five of the following factors is enough to indicate suicide potential and to alert the teacher that professional therapy may be needed:

> the student is male
> a past suicide attempt by a method other than ingestion
> more than one previous suicide attempt
> a history of antisocial behavior
> having a close friend who committed suicide
> having a family member who attempted suicide
> frequent drug or alcohol use
> depression
> friction between the youth and his home or school environment

The steps the nation's schools are taking in an effort to prevent suicide are varied. The goal of some educational systems is to prepare young people for a life free of self-generated illness—including depression, the underlying cause of much suicide. Classes in aerobics and jazzercise, jogging and yoga, slimnastics and weight training, low-calorie and sodium-free diets have become an important part of the new pedagogy, designed to help keep students physically and mentally healthy.

Teachers are driving home the message that preventive medicine makes good sense. They point out that the kind of life you choose today determines *if* you'll live tomorrow. They also remind students that when they're unfriendly to their bodies and their environment, the unfriendliness is returned in a vengeful way—usually through illness.

Educators who have picked up on the health-promotion

programs realize that modern school health education is not just hygiene, nor is it merely knowing the names of all the muscles and bones in the body. They are teaching more about first aid and CPR, rape prevention, chronic and communicable diseases, self-esteem, mental health, the environment, family life, sex education, nutrition and fitness, and substance abuse. Many of these topics are directly related to suicide. Lack of knowledge in any of these areas could lay the groundwork for physical and/or emotional problems in the future.

The school health program in Muscogee County, Georgia, is becoming a national model. In every classroom, from kindergarten to sixth grade, students spend an average of two hours each week on health-oriented topics. In grades seven to twelve, science, social studies, and home economics teachers direct the program. All courses in the curriculum emphasize the triad of physical, mental, and social health. More and more classes are including segments directly aimed at suicide prevention.

In addition to establishing new health and awareness programs, many schools are asking students to help each other by forming peer helper groups. Such support organizations are made up of students who are specially trained by school counselors to listen to fellow classmates and to assist with their problems by sharing their feelings and their advice. The peer helping concept is based on the idea that young people will talk about their problems more readily with classmates than with parents, teachers, or other adults.

These specially trained students learn to listen in a caring way to the problems other students may have concerning schoolwork, new-student adjustment, family relationships, death and dying, drugs and alcohol, and, more recently, suicide. Peer helpers take on a large responsibility. They often give up some of their after-school or weekend time to meet with fellow students and discuss problems.

Although peer helpers are specially trained in many areas, problems may arise that they feel uncomfortable with or that they can't handle. This is sometimes the case when a troubled student mentions suicidal feelings.

In such instances, the peer helper is asked to immediately alert an adult counselor or adviser, to inform the troubled student of additional places where he can turn to get more assistance, and to continue listening to him in a caring and friendly way.

Classroom teachers who blend ideas on suicide prevention with their regular curriculum are on the upswing. Some of them are using the study of Shakespeare's *Romeo and Juliet* in their English classes to encourage students to consider alternatives to suicide. Pupils are asked to present other ways in which the main characters might have dealt with their problems. Bookmarks suggesting other endings to the play are available through the Youth Suicide National Center, 1825 I Street, N.W., Suite 945, Washington, D.C. 20006.

Another thing schools are doing to prevent suicide involves cracking down on students who bring weapons to the campus. Sometimes one reads headlines about a youth carrying a gun or a knife into a classroom, killing a classmate or a teacher, then turning the weapon on himself. An Iowa school board drafted the following specific punishments to be meted out to weapon-bearing students: five days' suspension for possession of a weapon; ten days' suspension for displaying a weapon; suspension with a recommendation of expulsion for displaying any weapon in a threatening manner.

The administration at this school also maintains the right to search lockers whenever a reasonable suspicion exists that a weapon may be found. Tips most often come from other students.

All across the nation, schools are implementing the suicide-prevention measures they feel will be most effective in their educational systems.

In California, pilot programs have been started at the junior high and high school level to inform students about depression, feelings of despair, and the risk of self-inflicted death.

In Plano, Texas, schools, there is a support group for troubled teens as well as one for new students, which helps them develop friendships and adjust to the new school situation.

Psychologists in Clear Lake City, Texas, met with the high school's faculty and students to alert teachers and counselors to suicide warning signs.

After a second youth suicide in Mesa County, Colorado, school officials interviewed all students at a junior high school to identify teens who might be at risk. Mental-health professionals followed up by counseling twenty high-risk students.

More than three thousand New Jersey educators have been trained in a suicide-awareness program.

In Iowa's Nora Springs–Rock Falls Junior-Senior High School, principal Dick Lowery faced shocked parents and students after a teenager's suicide shook the district. The incident motivated Lowery to find out more about suicide. He learned about warning signals, statistics, and prevention programs; and then he shared his knowledge, often speaking to other school groups, community service clubs, and full assemblies of teenagers wondering about signs and symptoms to look for in their friends.

As the result of the death in Lowery's school, the district started covering suicide as part of its year-long sophomore health class. In the course, students learn to recognize signs that their friends might be thinking of suicide and what to do if they occur—namely, tell somebody. Follow-up programs are under way for juniors and seniors.

Lowery credits peer awareness of suicide potential for saving the lives of other students. "I've had several kids who've come to me and said they thought I should talk to a friend of theirs," Lowery said. Some have brought a friend's suicide note to him, asking for advice. Lowery talks with the potentially suicidal student and usually refers the youth for counseling or assessment.

The system of student awareness and referral is not foolproof by any means. Several years after the first suicide in Lowery's school, there was another. The aftermath of shock, denial, and anger was similar to that following the first suicide, and it was accompanied by even stronger feelings of guilt.

"Some of us, including myself, felt a deep disappointment that we had failed somewhere," Lowery said. "While it helps to know that other suicides have been averted, that in itself is not enough. Yes, we are doing something. But the fact is that there was a second suicide, and whatever we were doing was not enough in that case."

Many school administrators believe it is imperative to have some type of program set up within a school district that ensures orderly crisis management. Such structure is necessary for the staff as well as for the students. Not every teacher in a system is well suited to deal with a suicide situation. It is important for administrators to identify empathetic, effective communicators who handle pressure well, and to inform those people what is expected of them.

If a self-inflicted death has taken place, tension is relieved and chances of another such tragedy are lessened when the staff and the students talk together about what has happened. It is a good plan to downplay a suicide, but attempting a cover-up won't work.

School staff members need to be aware of how students may react to the suicide of a classmate. They may cry. They may laugh. They may hold a finger to their head and pull a mock trigger. None of those actions is abnormal, and they may be typical. Teachers can use these types of behavior in a positive way by making them the basis of discussions about how students are feeling.

Educators point out that it is unwise to hold services for a deceased student in the school building, where emotions may reach unhealthy peaks. The few days or weeks following a suicide are considered crucial periods in which other such deaths may occur. The anniversary of a suicide is also a high-risk day because emotions are rekindled by the memory of the occurrence.

No matter what suicide-prevention programs have been implemented in a school, mental-health experts have learned that graduation from high school is one of the most stressful passages for adolescents. Commencement can be a peak time for anguish and depression.

At a high school on Chicago's North Shore, two students killed themselves within three months of graduation. School officials reacted by developing a course called the Three Ds of College. The letters referred to disillusionment, doubt, and depression.

The course avoided the topic of suicide, instead focusing on what it would be like to go away to college. It pointed out that the teenager could experience disillusionment with new peers, who might have different values and different notions of privacy. It noted that the student away from home for the first time might feel doubts about being able to meet his own as well as his parents' expectations. The third D, depression, referred to the feelings of loss a young person might feel after moving away from family, friends, home, favorite teachers, and a loved neighborhood.

Each spring thousands of senior students listen to speeches given by the dignitaries of their communities or their state. These speakers try to help ease the neophyte into life after high school, whether the graduates involved are going to college or into the business world.

James P. Gannon, former editor of *The Des Moines Register*, gave the following address to one group of seniors. It contains much humor, as many good speeches do, but it also contains a serious but heartwarming message that can help lift the spirits of those who may be suffering from the three Ds. The speech deserves careful thought.

To the graduates: Life isn't high school
Dear graduating seniors:

When your principal asked me to be your commencement speaker, I tried to think of an excuse to reject the invitation. Unfortunately, I did not have a schedule conflict. I was free on Friday, May 30, and there was no plausible reason that I could not appear in the gymnasium of Oskaloosa Community Senior High School to give you a rousing send-off.

The trouble was, my heart wasn't in it. I have heard too

many commencement speeches. They generally are boring and predictable: The speaker must congratulate and flatter you, extol your accomplishments, raise your hopes, and promise that you can conquer the world if you try.

I am supposed to tell you that these are the best years of your lives. Well, they aren't. Life is a lot more tolerable after you stop worrying about acne, your next date, and whether you can have the family car on Friday night. Looking back, I've concluded that the high school years are a sort of purgatory to which teenagers are sentenced after the bliss of childhood. For the rest of your life, you will wonder whether you have been released to heaven or to hell. Adulthood will bring some of both.

Life is unpredictable. Nobody can say what will become of each of you, but I can safely assert one truth: Life isn't like high school. The years won't follow some script written in your class yearbook.

I am certain that there is one among you—someone that you all agree is a real dork—who in fifteen years will be the owner of a chain of hotels or the president of a big electronics company. This guy, who dresses weird and never had a date, will live in a mansion and marry a beauty queen. Another among you, who won this year's contest for Mr. Popularity, will be his gardener.

Then there is Miss Vivacious, the cheerleader with the pearly teeth who never knew a lonely Friday night in four years; she will live in a trailer court with three kids on welfare, wondering where the football hero that she married went after he was let out on parole.

All I am saying is that the roles assigned to you by the social arbiters of the youth culture will not last. The high school stereotypes will shatter. The Eternal Truths of the

How Schools Can Help

Teen Years will prove perishable. In a few years, your parents won't seem as dumb as they used to be. Loud music played at all waking hours will begin to lose its appeal. You will not need to spend most of your time at home on the telephone. You will discover the value of silence, and the utility of going to bed when you are tired.

None of this will happen fast. All this will creep up on you, slowly and subtly, in a way that will allow you to pretend that you are not changing, that only others are. Someday it will occur to you that high school kids aren't nearly as mature as you were at that age. This is a telltale sign that you are approaching thirty.

But do not fear maturity. Growing up has advantages. It will allow you to become an individual—to have your own ideas, opinions, tastes, and values. You will become more free to decide what is worth your time, effort, and emotional investment. You will be less inclined to follow the crowd, and more inclined to chart your own course. You will cease looking for parades to join. You will be comfortable walking alone, at your own pace, to your own destination.

This is the freedom that self-confidence can confer, but it comes slowly and painfully. You earn it by living. It is the interest paid on experience. It is the dividend credited to those who become comfortable with themselves—with who they are, what they do best, and where that effort will make some difference.

Every commencement address must contain a bit of advice, so here is mine: Know who you are, and be proud of it. You will grow out of being a teenager (thank God) but you will not grow out of your background—your family, your religion, your ethnicity, your hometown, your state. These are things that will define you, and if you are uncomfortable with any of them, you will struggle against your own identity and ultimately fail to earn self-confidence.

You ultimately may come to the happiest realization of all: that the best years of your life are the ones that lie immediately ahead, whatever your age—for they are the only years that you can still make better than the ones you've already lived. Use them well.

11

What's a Family to Do?

Prevention, obviously, is the main goal in coping with suicide, and while parents and siblings would seem to be the most likely people a troubled youth might turn to for help, this is not always the case. He may turn to a friend, or a teacher, or perhaps he'll turn to nobody at all. Since a problem must be recognized before it can be solved, it is of utmost importance that all family members be aware of the suicidal warning signals.

Many years ago, Pearl S. Buck wrote of the Chinese family custom of putting each child in charge of the happiness of another sibling. This idea has merit for families with several children. Through the use of such a plan, a family would be more aware of the thoughts and troubles of its members. While enjoying the status of being in charge, siblings would be encouraged to respond with sympathy and understanding to another's problems and to bring a troubled child's feelings to the attention of a parent.

One father, in relating how he came to grips with the fact that his son was seriously depressed, recognized worrisome developments in their family life. When he first noticed subtle changes in his son's behavior, he told himself that the boy was just going through a phase.

But it didn't pass. Instead, the changes in his son's behavior became more noticeable. Then concerned people began to call the family, reporting that they had seen the boy taking needless chances—driving recklessly, diving from cliffs into unknown waters, skiing in dangerous areas.

After that, this youth engaged in flamboyant dressing. This included wearing necklaces, earrings, eyeliner, and dressing like a punk rocker. At that time, he also rebelled against all household rules, and, although he had never dated before, he started going out with a half a dozen girls on a regular basis.

When the father took his son to a psychiatrist, he found that the boy was suicidal. Luckily, the doctor was able to help, and this youth is now on his way to recovery.

It is sometimes true that a young person hasn't learned, in the process of growing up, sufficient ways to cope with losses or anticipated losses. Since a child's first experiences usually involve family and family teachings, parents are sometimes blamed for the self-inflicted death of their child. But many things work together to create a suicidal situation. It's a mistake to ascribe responsibility for such behavior solely to parents.

Charlotte Ross, while heading San Mateo County's Suicide Prevention and Crisis Center in California, found that families with suicidal adolescents differed little from other families. There is a presumption that there has to be something abnormal or wrong with the suicidal young person as well as something abnormal or wrong with the youth's parents. Ross found, in the families that she worked with, that though the parents were not perfect, they were some of the nicest and most normal people she had ever met.

It is also a mistake to assume that suicidal youths have uncaring parents who never listen to them and who fail to communicate. Most normal adolescents usually withdraw into themselves in situations involving their troubles and their parents. Sometimes they don't know how to communicate in a meaningful way.

In the case of one teenager, whose younger sister found him hanging in the family garage, neither parents nor siblings realized how troubled the boy was.

"I feel guilty in admitting that after the initial shock of realizing my brother was dead, my first feeling was one of relief," this young woman said. "My younger sister and brother and I had lived in fear of him. Both Mom and Dad worked, and my mother was in poor health. As the oldest girl in the family, I felt it was my after-school job to keep the peace at all costs. I took care of the younger kids and got our supper started. My mom disliked coming home to problems.

"At the time all this was happening, I was fourteen and my older brother, Joe, was sixteen. I thought he was just a mean, ornery kid. Lots of my friends complained about their brothers, and I thought Joe's behavior was normal for an older, know-it-all boy. He had a violent temper. If the rest of us would tease him, even mildly, or look at him in a way he didn't like, he would go into a rage.

"We would run for the bathroom, the only room in the house with a lock on the door. We'd cower there while he pounded on that door, fearful that he might actually break it down. I have scars on my hands and arms from the wounds my brother sometimes inflicted, but when my folks would ask about my injuries, I would cover for Joe, saying that the cuts and bruises were the result of accidents.

"I realize now that Joe's behavior was abnormal and that I had done him no favor by maintaining the peace and by keeping his actions a secret from my mom and dad. Had they known the extremes of his rages, they could have sought help for him. Even though I didn't know any better at the time, I'll always carry those guilt feelings about my brother's death."

This young woman was not unique in her ignorance of the warning signals that can point to a suicidal person. And even when parents or siblings are aware of these signals, they may be perplexed. What family has children who aren't moody? What family has children who never put themselves down or compare themselves unfavorably with their friends? What family has children whose eating and sleeping patterns never fluctuate? Many young people have at some time or other looked at a bad grade on a test paper or on a report card, slapped their foreheads, and jokingly said, "I think I'll end it all."

A family may believe that such behavior is the norm. Psychiatrists point out that to some extent this may be true, but they warn that it's the degree of such behavior that may point to trouble ahead. They advise families to be on the lookout for and to observe carefully excessive actions of any kind.

Families don't always attach enough significance to what appear to them to be minor reverses in a young person's life. They can be blind to a youth's problems. New York psychiatrist Herbert Hendin cites an extreme example of a high school girl who slashed her wrists twice. Her wrists were badly scarred, and the scars were easily visible to anyone who looked at her arms.

The girl always took pains to wear short-sleeved dresses to the family dinner table, but her mother and father never questioned the scars. They made no comments. Sometimes she would even wear bandages around her wrists; yet her parents never asked what the bandages were for. This girl was lucky. A third suicide attempt with pills resulted in her being taken to a hospital, where she ultimately received the psychiatric help that saved her life.

When a young person who usually earns straight A's gets a B, it is upsetting. When a youth fails to make the team, the cheering squad, or some special group that he has his heart set on, it hurts. These people are searching for someone who cares that they're suffering.

An adult or a sibling may be oblivious to the extent of another family member's need. He might shrug off similar reverses in his own life, but to a teenager who is inexperienced in coping with setbacks, such failures might trigger suicidal ideas.

Mental-health experts suggest that the first step is to try to find out how the troubled person is feeling. Ask. If a youth refuses to discuss his glum feelings, and if he still seems sad, it's a good idea for family members to question his friends. Have you noticed that Hank seems rather depressed lately? Do you know why Suzie feels so down? Such questions may result in answers that will give clues to a youth's problems. There are many things parents can do to help a child before serious depression sets in and the child becomes suicidal. They must be ready to accept the idea that their child may be depressed and that he may need the care of a mental-health expert. It may be hard to accept this idea, but to deny it is to let the problem develop unchecked.

A parent who has reason to suspect his offspring is suicidal should find professional help for that child immediately. One East Coast mother wishes she had done just that. Her son, whom we'll call Jack, was an athlete, and things in his world were going poorly. His mother first noticed a change in her son when she visited his campus in late August.

Football practice had already started and Jack complained, "Mom, you can't believe how they treat us. They don't care if you give two hundred percent. They want more."

Jack had never been a complainer. His words were ominous, but even more chilling for his mother was the sight of his tears. Jack seldom cried. His mother was unsure of how to help, so she did nothing. In a subsequent game, Jack was injured. He spent most of the season on the bench. Late the next summer, when Jack and his mother started talking about school, Jack cried again about his disappointing athletic career. He seemed very depressed.

"Jack, are you suicidal?" his mother asked.

"If August tenth hadn't been your birthday, I would have blown my brains out on August ninth," he replied.

Mother and son had a long talk, and she suggested that he see a counselor, but she didn't follow the suggestion with action. And Jack didn't heed her advice. A week later, Jack fatally shot himself. Perhaps even with counseling this death could not have been prevented, but that mother will always blame herself for failing to find a counselor for Jack and for failing to see that he set up and kept his appointment.

Many young people balk at the idea of therapy. Who

needs it? Who wants it? But regardless of a youth's wishes, it is important for a parent not only to find a counselor but also to find one to whom the troubled person can relate. One mother let her son abandon counseling sessions when he told her he hated the therapist and could never relate to him. She never thought to look for another doctor whom the boy would like and with whom he could get along. Her son killed himself a short time later.

It isn't difficult to find a qualified therapist. A parent can seek such information from a family physician, a friend who may have been involved in a similar situation, a member of the clergy, or a teacher.

Treatment for suicide attempters usually involves psychotherapy and family therapy. Until recently, giving antidepressants to adolescents was unusual, but the use of such medication has become much more common within the past five years. Parents are well advised to consider treatment for suicidal tendencies a long-term process. But with expert help, there is good reason to hope for recovery.

In addition to seeking counseling for a troubled offspring, parents also can help by making more room in their lives for their child's ideas and activities, by putting their own concerns second to his.

Listen. While adults make time to hear what their offspring have to say, they should be aware that they need to keep an open mind, and they should be sure to allow for differences of opinion.

It's important for parents to be aware of their own actions as they relate to those of their children. They should ask themselves if they are trying to guide the young person in a direction that is wrong for him. For example, a mother who as a teenager was shy and retiring may try to relive her life in fantasy by pressing her daughter to be popular and vivacious. Or a father who was always an athletic hero may expect his son to follow in his footsteps. Such expectations and pressures can be hard on a youth whose natural bent directs him to a different course of action.

Communication between parent and offspring is most important. It is the responsibility of the adult to keep the lines of communication open, even if the youth turns away. The grown-ups are the authority figures in a family. If they quit trying to talk to their children, they are being irresponsible.

Another important thing a mother or father can do is to communicate and cooperate with the child's teacher. It has been said that kings sometimes killed messengers who brought bad tidings. Parents cannot afford to let themselves resent the teacher who may point out their child's negative actions. That teacher can be one of a family's strongest supporters.

Perhaps the most important thing an adult can do for a troubled offspring is to be open to outside help, which may come from a family doctor or from a psychiatrist or a psychologist. Prevention is the main objective when dealing with a suicidal teenager. There is a lot family members can do, and their actions can be lifesaving.

12

The Role of Church and Community

Whenever a youth dies of self-inflicted injuries, a whole area suffers. Community grief is compounded by guilt and confusion. People experience a heightened awareness of the briefness of life. They also harbor a sense of hopelessness when it comes to coping with the suicide, and they often turn to church and community for solace and assistance.

The city of Glastonbury, Connecticut, offers a good example of cooperation between church, school, and community to prevent self-inflicted deaths among its young people. In 1985, following the suicide of a local college student and several attempts by other young people, the Conference of Churches in Glastonbury teamed up with the city's Youth and Family Services, Glastonbury High School, and the Glastonbury Visiting Nurses to present a series of programs aimed at suicide prevention.

The timing of the presentation was important. The program developers wanted to present their ideas before a crisis occurred. Because spring is a high-risk period for teenagers, they chose to begin their effort by fitting the topic of suicide into church sermons on All Souls Sunday in early November.

The program then continued with the distribution of specially written brochures in the high school and junior high school and the development of plans on how to present anti-suicide ideas to youth groups in the community.

In planning these events, church people felt that they needed to explore their own stances on suicide. To begin this process of reflection, a core group presented area ministers with a packet of reference material and a list of pertinent Bible passages. The goal was not to reach a consensus of opinion on suicide, but simply to address a difficult theological issue that many people avoid until they are faced with a crisis.

Two weeks before All Souls Sunday, material for a bulletin insert was sent to all churches. It included the warning signs of suicide, what to do to try and prevent this tragedy, and emergency telephone numbers to call in the event of a crisis. On that Sunday, ministers either addressed the subject of suicide in their sermons or at least acknowledged it through announcement, a moment of concern, or a special reading.

The principal secular event in the program took place on that Sunday evening, when an ecumenical cast of young people presented the play *Quiet Cries*. This production was from the Plays for Living series written and produced under the auspices of the Family Service Association of America.

In the play, three characters contemplate committing suicide for quite different reasons. Although it is indicated at the beginning of the drama that one of the three characters will actually take his life, the story is open-ended. The audience must decide who the victim is. Leaders divided the audience into discussion groups led by social workers, counselors, and nurses, and a lively debate followed the performance.

Everyone who saw the play was asked to write down personal feelings about the evening. One viewer wrote, "I'm glad I came tonight, because talking with a group of parents and kids that really understand was helpful. I'm going to get help for my best friend."

Another person commented, "I found out how to know when people are having trouble. I also learned how to help others. To me, it proved that people really do care, and that's really good to know."

Following the program, a counselor from Youth and Family Services was available to speak with anyone who felt the need to talk privately right then.

Part of the reason for directing the program at people who wanted to learn how to help their friends was to provide the necessary cover for youths who might need help themselves. No one asked for help that night, but during the next two weeks, nurses at the high school saw an increase in the number of young people wanting to talk about their suicidal feelings.

The planners of the Glastonbury program realized that a single effort, no matter how strong, would have only a temporary effect on the thinking and actions of the participants. They continued to search for other programs that could be used in the high school and junior high or as part of church youth fellowships. They planned to present another play that fall, and they offered ideas for starting a peer counseling group in the schools.

In some communities, the Young Women's Christian Association indirectly approaches the topic of suicide in its new life-options program called Choices or Chances. This program, using a board-game format, is designed to help involve young people in a role-playing discussion of personal issues. The game may be played by a group of ten to fourteen young people, ages fourteen and up, or by a group of parents.

Each player is assigned a character with a specific background, along with the attendant attributes and problems of that character. The players select and read aloud cards that describe situations or questions facing their characters. Discussions, decisions, and consequences all follow, as each participant enacts two to three years of decision making in his or her character's life.

The made-up situations in the game cover a wide variety of topics that represent the kinds of issues that young people may face today in our society: peer and parental relationships, health issues, drug use, loss of a loved one. Human sexuality has been included because it is considered to be a crucial part of a young person's physical and emotional growth. Many of these issues relate either directly or indirectly to the problem of suicide.

The topics presented are intended to foster learning by correcting false ideas and by providing new and accurate information. It is also a goal of the program to provide youths with decision-making opportunities in an attempt to increase their skill in making informed decisions.

A specially trained adult conducts this YWCA program. Her job includes verifying the facts and information shared, drawing out underlying values the teens already possess, creating an environment that is comfortable and fun for the participants, guiding discussions to make sure all aspects of a question are aired, and promoting the social and psychological well-being of each girl.

After participating in this life-options program, young people are encouraged to discuss some of the topics with their parents. However, the game is designed to enhance family communication, not to replace it. More information on this life-options program is available from the Young Women's Christian Association, 726 Broadway, New York, New York 10003.

A practical program designed to help both troubled youths and the elderly has been implemented by an Iowa community. Young people from New Providence's Quakerdale Home, a private, nonprofit residential treatment center for predelinquent and delinquent adolescents, are teaming up with residents of Valley View Nursing Home in Eldora. They bridge the gap between generations by caring and sharing.

A program called Helping Hands brings these people together. Surprising as it may seem, there are problems common to both troubled youths and nursing home residents. Both groups are experiencing institutional care, and both groups often feel that they have lost control of their lives and are being forced to rely on others. For the youths, feelings of depression, hopelessness, and unimportance often lead to acts of destruction and aggression against others as well as against themselves. For the nursing home residents, similar feelings lead to withdrawal and dejection.

In trying to help both the elderly and the young, social workers try to uncover strong feelings that are seldom spoken. The elderly, who have survived two world wars and a great depression, are not inclined to wear their hearts on their sleeves. But neither are delinquent kids, who form a subculture where emotional warmth and sharing are considered weaknesses. Troubled teenagers may be overburdened with strong feelings: anger toward abusive parents, fears about their future, pain, and loneliness.

Once a week at the nursing home, the two groups get together to share their problems and to help each other work them out. They are encouraged to honestly express strong emotions and to respond sensitively to the feelings of others. Talking and listening work for these people.

One boy said, "If I come here with a bad attitude, they turn me around to a good positive attitude. I learn to bring out some feelings."

One social worker involved in the Helping Hands program pointed out the great impact the meetings have had on the transmission of values from one generation to the next. The program preaches values; it makes values fashionable. Confusion regarding their personal value system is a key problem to many troubled teenagers. They may be responding to inconsistent messages and poor modeling in their families. In the Helping Hands group, these supposedly resistive youngsters will hungrily absorb common-sense advice about living, along with moral lectures from the nursing home residents.

The program is not all talk and listening. There's action involved too. Cooking sessions are very popular. The group has cooked Chinese food, Mexican dishes, and even bear stew. One of the older residents looked at a taco and said if he ate something like that, the kids had to try bear meat. And so they did.

An analysis of the Helping Hands project shows that the members of the group are feeling better about themselves because they are reaching out to one another. Caring and sharing form the foundation of this program, and it works.

Some community health-care agencies have implemented music therapy as an additional service to help troubled patients who may be depressed, mentally ill, or users of alcohol and drugs. This therapy uses the process of making music—singing, improvising, playing, writing, creating, and performing—to improve a patient's social, emotional, cognitive, or communication skills.

A Louisiana musical therapist gives a brief case history of one young adult who had made several attempts on her life and who found help through music therapy. This young woman was two when her parents divorced. She was sexually molested by her stepfather as a child and a teenager. At nineteen she married a drug addict, bore a child, and then was divorced. Her life experiences ran the gamut from heavy drinking and drug involvement to marrying an undeclared homosexual. Her self-directed aggression resulted in her being admitted to a psychiatric hospital where, in addition to usual health care, she also received music therapy in the form of guitar lessons.

At first, she used the guitar as an outlet for her emotions, but as her therapy sessions progressed, she gradually realized that what she really needed was someone to talk to. She recognized the fact that she had never had a life for herself or time to find out what she wanted from life.

Gradually she became aware of the many options available to her. Slowly she began to show confidence in herself. Her progress was not all straight ahead. She was frightened by recurring suicidal thoughts, but at the same time she was encouraged by the developing bond between herself and her musical therapist.

One day, as a special surprise for her therapist, she played a program of several songs. She also agreed to sign a support-system contract, in which she promised that after her release from the hospital she would call that hospital if and when she felt suicidal. Without music therapy, her prognosis might not have been as good.

Perhaps the most prevalent antisuicide campaigns are similar to the one being used in Plano, Texas. After the cluster of self-induced deaths in that city, citizens collected $150,000 in community donations to set up a crisis center and to support a hot line for potential suicides. At the same time, local churches strengthened family activities, youth counseling, and programs aimed at educating people about suicide.

Today, as a result of similar programs and campaigns, there are many ways for a troubled person to find help in a crisis situation. Many cities and towns offer a twenty-four-hour, seven-day-a-week emergency telephone service designed to give aid quickly. Some communities have their own rescue squads to assist people after they've taken an overdose, shot themselves, or slit their wrists. Other communities have telephone hookups to emergency services so they can summon help quickly.

Mental-health clinics in most cities are listed in the Yellow Pages of the telephone directory under Mental Health. If such listings cannot be found, a person can receive emergency help by dialing 0 or 911, or by calling the police, a local hospital, or the fire department.

Churches and communities are helping prove that suicide can be prevented.

13

The National and International Scene

Since suicide among young people is a widespread problem, national and international organizations have been established to help combat it. In 1774 in England, the Royal Humane Society was created to deter attempted suicides. In 1906 in New York, the National-Save-a-Life League became the first suicide-prevention agency in this country.

The idea of a prevention center is not new. It is the proliferation of these centers that is new. Today, if services that are strictly telephone hot lines are considered, there are about 700. In 1960 there were fewer than half a dozen.

One older and effective organization that addresses the problem of suicide is the Samaritans. Dedicated to helping troubled people, the Samaritan organization was founded in England about thirty-five years ago. This is a nonreligious and nonprofessional service that offers a listening ear rather than counseling. In the United States, this group's offices are listed in the telephone directory, usually in the white pages.

Trained volunteers man Samaritan phone lines and listen to the troubled person without being judgmental and without offering quick solutions or unwanted advice. These volunteers are backed up by professional counselors, and they trace no calls and take no action unless it is requested. Everything they hear and say is confidential. Workers for this organization report that about one-third of the callers mention suicide and stress in their first conversation. The Samaritans are there to help.

In 1984, a group of parents of children who had taken their lives approached former New York state Lieutenant Governor Alfred B. DelBello to discuss the tragedy of youth suicide, its epidemic proportions, and the lack of government response to the situation. Investigation by the lieutenant governor's staff found the need for an organized and coordinated approach to the problem. As an outgrowth of these findings, the National Committee on Youth Suicide Prevention (NCYSP) was established and incorporated in 1985.

The chief purpose of this nonprofit organization is to reduce the number of committed and attempted suicides among our nation's youth. The plan to accomplish this involves working to increase public awareness of the problem, encouraging new prevention programs, and supporting research and evaluation efforts. Over forty-five state chapters of the NCYSP have been established to monitor the incidence of youth suicide within their states. These chapters disseminate prevention information and focus public attention on the need for a federal commission to study the national scope of youthful self-destruction.

The NCYSP acts as a national clearinghouse. It provides information and referrals to prevention groups and organizations in every part of the country, enabling them to share ideas and insights that can mean the difference between life and death.

This organization is also developing for national distribution a series of youth suicide brochures and a resource guide listing referral agencies, information services, and lay groups with a special interest in this subject. In addition, it provides the names, addresses, and telephone numbers of specialists who conduct mental-health evaluations of adolescents thought to be at risk of suicide.

A directory that includes a comprehensive listing of approximately a thousand suicide prevention and crisis intervention services is available from the NCYSP. This directory includes agencies and programs in all fifty states and the District of Columbia. It can be ordered for $3.00 per copy from the National Committee on Youth Suicide Prevention, 67 Irving Place South, New York, New York 10033.

The year 1985 also marked the establishment of the Youth Suicide National Center (YSNC). This nonprofit organization has offices at 1825 I Street N.W., Suite 945, Washington, D.C. 20006 and at 1811 Trousdale Drive, Burlingame, California 94010.

In response to concerned citizens, the YSNC works at both the local and national level, serving as an information clearinghouse. It also develops and distributes educational materials, coordinates a national awareness campaign, provides educational programs and related services, and supports and encourages self-help groups and services for survivors.

This center, under the direction of Charlotte P. Ross, is reviewing current youth suicide-prevention programs and developing models that can be responsive to the needs of diverse groups in communities across the country. Its leaders hope to establish a national toll-free hot line to respond to depressed and suicidal youth and their families.

For a nominal charge, YSNC will provide brochures for both students and school personnel titled "Suicide in Youth and What You Can Do about It," a suggested reading list for teenagers, and an audiovisual resource list.

One of the most recent national programs that may be indirectly related to suicide prevention is being implemented by the Ford Foundation. Sometimes a suicidal youth is either a school dropout or a student seriously considering dropping out. The Ford Foundation has begun a nationwide effort to prevent school dropouts by matching students prone to quit school with aid that would address their particular problems.

The foundation, which estimates that 25 percent of all high school students fail to graduate, plans to spend $1.1 million in twenty-one city school districts and to encourage collaboration between school and community leaders in the program. In some cities the dropout rate among black and Hispanic students is said to range as high as 60 to 80 percent. Since young black males have one of the highest suicide rates in the nation, the Ford program is indirectly speaking to this area of concern.

Nationally and internationally, dedicated people continue efforts to reduce the incidence of youth suicide. In 1985, rock singer Billy Joel donated all royalties from "You're Only Human," from his album *Billy Joel's Greatest Hits,* volumes 1 and 2 (Columbia), to the National Committee for Youth Suicide Prevention. He said he was doing it because the teenage son of a close business associate had committed suicide, and he indicated that he himself had considered suicide in his youth.

While it is true that dedicated people continue their efforts to reduce the incidence of youth suicide, many mental-health experts are realizing that some prevention programs are failing to reach the young people who are most at risk—youths who are alienated from friends, family, and school. Dropouts and runaways seldom seek help through traditional channels.

In addressing this problem, Diane Ryerson of New Jersey's South Bergen Mental Health Center says, "We need to work more closely with police, probation departments, rock music stations, record stores—and bartenders."

As more people begin to work together to combat the problem of youth suicide, potential victims have a much better chance of receiving lifesaving help.

14

You Are Stronger Than You Think

It is quite possible that a person who is thinking of taking his life may be reading this book. If you are such a person, please read this chapter closely.

You may think nobody listens to you, that nobody cares, that your friends and parents are devoted to giving you a bad time. You may feel confused about sex and sexuality, be involved in drugs, or be under too much pressure. You may see no way out of your troubles.

But you don't really want to die.

What you want is to be able to stop the pain of living. You're hurting, and nobody seems to understand. You can't imagine a time when the hurting will stop. Although you may find it hard to believe, your problems will lessen and, given time, they will clear up.

Hang on.

Don't act impulsively. You may have bitter feelings toward adults who say that young people act without thinking. Suicidal thoughts build up over a period of weeks, months, and even years. However, some therapists believe that the suicidal crisis—that period of time in which a person actually decides to pull the trigger or swallow the pills or tighten the noose—usually lasts about ten minutes.

Ten minutes.

If you can force yourself to live through those ten agonizing minutes, you'll have a chance to take a clearheaded look at your problems and to turn your life around. You'll have the option of living a full life. Don't deny yourself this opportunity.

You are stronger than you think.

Remember one important thing. Killing yourself is a permanent solution to a temporary problem. Yes, your problems are temporary. You *can* get your family to communicate with you. You *can* find another girlfriend or boyfriend. You *can* bear being excluded from your favorite "in" group. Failing grades *can* be brought up to the passing level. A brush with the law *can* be worked out in the courts. These things may be difficult to accomplish, but *you can do it.*

Try simple solutions first. They may not work, but try them before you go on to something more complex and final. If you went to a doctor complaining of a stomachache, and he said, "That's too bad. Guess we'll have to take out your appendix," you probably would question his methods. You might have expected the doctor to assume the ache was only temporary and to try less permanent solutions first. Surely you would have expected him to take your temperature, to inquire what you had eaten in the past few hours, to ask if you had been exposed to the flu, to prescribe some medication that might lessen the pain until he had time to do some tests and to make a more thorough diagnosis.

If you find yourself in a suicidal crisis, hang on for ten minutes or so. Of course you can. You must. When the crisis period is behind you, then it's time to do what a good doctor would. Try some simple solutions to your problems first. You may be saying that you've already tried everything and nothing has worked for you.

Don't give up. Hang on. And while you're hanging on, find a pen and paper.

Make a list. You may be feeling that you're such a bad person and total failure that the world would be better off without you. These feelings are probably so strong that they're blotting out your memory of the good things about you. To help you keep a better mental balance, start writing a list of your good points. You have them. And you know what they are. Write them down. You may not think of many at first, but given time and thought, your list will grow. When you are searching for answers as to why you should go on living, refer to this list. The reasons are there. The world needs people with your good qualities.

Other chapters in this book have told you what friends and family can do to help you. You've read what schools, community, and the nation can do to assist in keeping you alive. Now it's time to consider what you can do for yourself. By this time, you have safely survived those crucial ten minutes. They are behind you. You've even made a list of your good points.

Now it's time to reach out to others. Talk to someone. You may be thinking that you've already tried that. And failed. You can't talk to your parents. They don't have time to listen. Your school counselor said to come back next week, fourth period. Your friends just laughed and said, "Snap out of it. What are you wearing to the dance Saturday night?" The minister? You could never talk to him.

Rest assured that there are people who will listen as well as talk to you about your problems. Dial 0, or dial 911 and ask for the number of a suicide-crisis center. Then call that number. You'll probably notice that you're feeling a bit better already because you're taking strong action on your own behalf.

Someone who wants to help you will answer your call and listen to what you have to say. That person will not condemn you. Or laugh. Or run off before you've really reached the point of your message. That person will listen no matter how long you talk or how many times you call back.

You'll have your helper's first name, and you can even ask for him or her personally the next time you telephone. Or you can ask him to call you at a certain time and place. This person has a sincere desire to help you. Don't deny him the privilege.

Now that you've established contact with someone who wants to assist you, there are other things you can do to help yourself. Rejoin the world. You've probably been feeling so down and depressed that you've holed up in your room, seeing few other people as you devote full time to worrying about your problems.

Again, this won't be easy, but you must leave your room. Leave your house. Rejoin your former friends and take part in some group activities. If you need to work into this slowly, you might begin by just taking a solo walk around your neighborhood. Getting out and about will help you break the worrying pattern you've established.

Mingling and talking with others isn't going to make your troubles vanish overnight. Don't expect that. But you will probably find that you feel more calm and more able to analyze your situation in a rational way.

Think back to your last happy gift-giving season when you bought or made presents for your family. You probably wrapped those gifts, wrote tags for them, and personally presented them to the recipients. But you didn't accomplish this task all at once.

In all likelihood, you broke the gift-giving problem into segments by making a list, jotting down what each person on your list might like, then deciding if you should make or purchase that special item. This step-by-step process is a good system for analyzing any important problem.

Break the worries that have been overwhelming you down into smaller parts. If you feel you're failing in school, analyze your position in each class you're taking. Is it book reports that are holding you back in English class? Is lab work your nemesis in chemistry? Pinpoint the trouble areas; then set about doing something about them. Don't hesitate to call upon your teachers for help.

This suggestion may seem like an oversimplification, but most problems can be broken down into smaller parts that you can handle. *You are stronger than you think.*

One of the most important things you can do for yourself is to seek professional guidance. Your parents can assist you in finding a therapist, and that counselor's help may be the big breakthrough you've been seeking and needing.

The girl and boy who told their stories in this book both agreed that their suicidal crises took place in about ten minutes. Both were glad that their attempts to take their lives were unsuccessful. They're happy that they're alive. Neither youth is leading a trouble-free life, but both of them have found that by trying to help themselves and by reaching out to others, they have diminished their own problems. Both credit a part of their present well-being to the help of professional therapists.

Michelle is working in a day-care center, helping children

as she waits to enter college. Sam spends his summers working with children as a camp counselor and hopes to return to his second year of college in the fall. These two would-be suicide victims found and used their potential strengths.

You can too.

Reference Materials

BOOKS: NONFICTION

Alvarez, A. *The Savage God: A Study of Suicide.* New York: Random House, 1972.

Bolton, Iris, and Mitchell Curtis. *My Son . . . My Son.* Atlanta, Georgia: Bolton Press, 1983.

Griffin, Mary, and Carol Felsenthal. *A Cry for Help.* New York: Doubleday & Company, 1983.

Hafen, Brent Q., and Kathryn J. Frandsen. *Youth Suicide: Depression & Loneliness.* Colorado: Cordillera Press, 1986.

Kolehmainen, Janet, and Sandra Handwerk. *Teen Suicide.* Minneapolis, Minnesota: Lerner Publications Company, 1986.

Kunz, Roxane Brown, and Judy Harris Swenson. *Feeling Down: The Way Back Up.* Minneapolis, Minnesota: Dillon Press, 1986.

Langone, John. *Dead End: A Book About Suicide.* Boston: Little Brown, 1986.

Lee, Essie E., and Richard Wortman, M.D. *Down Is Not Out.* New York: Julian Messner, 1986.

Madison, Arnold. *Suicide & Young People.* New York: The Seabury Press, 1978.

Powledge, Fred. *You'll Survive.* New York: Scribners, 1986.

BOOKS: FICTION

Green, Hannah. *I Never Promised You a Rose Garden.* New York: Holt, 1964.

Guest, Judith. *Ordinary People.* New York: Viking Press, 1976.

PERIODICALS

Amdur, Nell. "Can an Athlete Take Fitness Too Far?" *Seventeen* (July 1983): 24–26.

Anonymous. "I Wanted to Die." *Reader's Digest* (July 1987): 93–96.

Demak, Richard. "And Then She Just Disappeared." *Sports Illustrated* (June 16, 1986): 18–19.

Englebardt, Stanley L. "It Can Be Prevented." *Reader's Digest* (July 1987): 97–98.

Hendin, Herbert, M.D. "Suicide: A Review of New Directions in Research." *Hospital and Community Psychiatry,* vol. 37, no. 2 (February 1986): 148–153.

Jacoby, Susan. "How to Help a Friend in Trouble." *Glamour* (May 1986): 292, 293–295, 355–357.

Martz, Larry. "The Copycat Suicides." *Newsweek* (March 23, 1987): 28–29.

Richman, Alan. "A 16-Year-Old Alabama Boy Points a Gun, Shoots a Friend and Kills Himself in Remorse." *People* (January 13, 1986): 45–48.

Ubell, Earl. "Is That Child Bad—or Depressed?" *Parade* (November 2, 1986).

Wilentz, Amy. "Teen Suicide." *Time* (March 23, 1987): 12–13.

EDUCATIONAL FILMS AND VIDEOTAPES

Did Jenny Have to Die? Pleasantville, New York: Sunburst Communications, Room SJ6, 39 Washington Ave., 10570, 1980. Videotape.

Suicide: But Jack Was a Good Driver. Del Mar, California: McGraw-Hill Training Systems, Box 641, 674 Via de la Valle, 92014, 1974. Videotape or film.

Suicide: It Doesn't Have to Happen. New York: BFA Educational Media, 468 Park Avenue South, 10016, 1976. Videotape or film.

Suicide: The Warning Signs. Chicago: Centron Films, 65 East S. Water St., 60601. Videotape or film.

Teens Who Chose Life: The Suicidal Crisis. Pleasantville, New York: Sunburst Communications, Room SJ6, 39 Washington Ave., 10570, 1986. Videotape.

Information concerning additional up-to-the-minute research sources on suicide and suicide prevention is available from the following consulting firm:

H-F Associates
Technical Information Resources
P.O. Box 19254
Houston, Texas 77224-9254
(713) 461-6789

Index

accidents, 6, 26, 42, 43
acquired immune deficiency syndrome (AIDS), 32
aggression, 5, 107, 109
alcohol, serotonin and, 25
alcohol abuse, 12, 23, 30–31, 43, 54, 84, 85, 86, 109
alienation, 9, 115
All Souls Sunday, 103–104
Alsip, Ill., 42
American Association of Suicidology (AAS), 82
American Journal of Psychiatry, 35
American Psychiatric Association, 25, 39
Amish, Old Order of, 23–24
angel dust, 29
anger, 32, 36–37, 47, 72, 74, 79, 89, 108
antidepressants, 44, 69, 101
anxiety, 34, 76

Archives of General Psychiatry, 14
Aristotle, 6
Arizona, suicide rate in, 12
Asberg, Marie, 24
atonement, 21–22
attention, need for, 4, 13, 18, 22, 46, 66–67
Augustine, Saint, 7

bartenders, 115
basuco, 29–30
behavior:
  antisocial, 51, 68, 70, 85
  disturbing and disruptive, 13–14, 53, 61, 75, 85, 95–98, 107
  reverses in, 95–96, 98–99, 100
  unreasonable risks in, 13–14, 37, 38, 75, 96
  violent, 13, 51, 53–54, 97–98

behavior, *cont'd.*
see also warning signs
Bergen County, N.J., 84, 115
Bergenfield, N.J., 32, 42–43, 84
birth factors, 20
blacks, statistics on, 11, 114
Blackstone, Sir William, 8
body language, 54–55
boredom, 35, 53, 55
boyfriends, *see* romances
brain, chemical abnormalities of, 24–26, 32, 39–40
Bryan High School, 44, 45
Buck, Pearl S., 95

California, suicide-prevention program in, 88
carbon monoxide poisoning, 42, 43, 44
caring, need for, 18, 29, 66, 82, 99, 105, 107, 109, 116
Carstensen, Lundie L., 27
Centers for Disease Control, 6, 11, 42
Cheyenne, Wyo., 41, 46
Chicago, Ill., 42, 90
Choices or Chances, 106–107
Christian teachings, 7
churches, 68, 103, 104, 105, 110
Clear Lake City, Tex., 41, 43–44, 88

clergymen, 38, 68, 79, 101, 104, 118
cluster suicides, 41–48, 83, 90, 110
cocaine, 29, 30, 43, 62
communication, 97, 107, 109, 117
confusion, 18–19, 50, 103, 108, 116
Connecticut, suicide rate in, 11
Council of Orleans, 7
counselors, counseling, *see* psychologists, psychiatrists
crack, 29, 30
crime, 12, 23, 51, 117
crisis centers, *see* suicide-prevention centers
cult worship, 14

death of loved ones, 21, 22, 36
dejection, 33, 37, 107
DelBello, Alfred B., 112
delinquency, 12, 51, 107–108, 117
depression, 8, 13, 33–40
  behavior changes and, 50, 55, 84, 95–96, 99–100
  causes for, 15, 22, 32, 36–38, 54, 79, 85, 90–91
  childhood attachments and, 47
  clinical or major, 35,

depression, *cont'd.*
  36–38, 39, 69–70
  definitions of, 33, 35–36
  high school graduation and, 90–91
  intensity of, 33–36
  mild, 34–35, 36
  scientific research on, 24–25, 39–40
  statistics on, 33
  symptoms of, 14, 16, 35–36, 53, 107
  treatment for, 29, 38–40, 76–77, 85, 88, 109, 113, 119–120
  winter, 34–35
Des Moines, Iowa, 16
Des Moines Register, 91
despair, 9, 32, 65, 75, 88
Detroit, Mich., 26
disillusionment, 90, 91
divorce, 45, 60, 70, 109
DNA, 39
doubt, 90, 91
dropouts, 37, 43, 44, 60, 62, 114, 115
drowning, 42
drug abuse, 12, 23, 29–31, 32, 54, 58, 62, 63, 75, 81, 83, 84, 85, 86, 106, 109, 116
Drug Abuse Warning Network, 30
Drug Enforcement Administration, U.S., 29–30
Dulit, Everett, 13

eating habits, 52, 56, 75, 98
education, on suicide, 83–95, 103–110
Education, U.S. Department of, 29
Egeland, Janice, 23, 39
elderly, 5, 9, 23, 33, 107–108
Eldora, Iowa, 107
emotional pain, 78, 108, 116
energy, 35
England, 8, 111
euthanasia, 9
expectations, living up to, 71, 91, 101–102

Fairview, Pa., 45
families, 95–102
  behavior reverses in, 95–96, 98–99, 100
  communication in, 97, 107, 117
  concern of, 10, 95–96, 98–100
  counseling for, 38–39, 101
  disruptive behavior in, 13–14, 61, 85, 95–98
  dual-career, 45, 65
  financial considerations of, 5, 38
  loss in, 21, 22, 36, 47, 91, 96, 106
  potential victims and, 49, 108, 115, 118, 119
  problems in, 12, 59–63, 86, 97
  reactions of, 5, 8, 28

families, *cont'd.*
  suicidal members of, 12, 51, 85; *see also* heredity
  warning signs and, 51–52, 53, 95, 98
Family Service Association of America, 104
fatigue, 54
fire department, 110
5-hydroxyindoleacetic acid (5-HIAA), 24
Florida, 29
Ford Foundation, 114
Fowler, Richard, 30–31
France, 8
Freud, Sigmund, 5, 22–23
Frevert, Rita, 46
friends, 28, 73–82
  being there for, 76, 80, 81–82
  cluster suicides of, 12, 16, 22, 41–48, 83, 85, 90, 110
  determining seriousness of situation for, 80–81
  empathizing with, 77–79
  fear and courage of, 76, 80, 87
  listening to, 77, 82, 86–87
  parents and, 76, 78, 80, 95, 98, 99, 101
  potential victims and, 4–5, 115, 116, 118, 119
  problem solving with, 79–80, 82
  professional help for, 79–80, 82, 87

friends, *cont'd.*
  secrecy of, 80, 82
  soul-searching and guilt of, 74–75, 89
  taking action for, 81–82
  taking careful look at, 75–76
  talking with, 76–77, 82
  warning signs and, 50, 51, 53, 56, 73–82, 105
frustration, 15, 19, 45

Gannon, James P., 91
genes, defective, 39
Georgia, 86
girlfriends, *see* romances
Glastonbury, Conn., 103
Goodwin, Guy, 25
Gould, Madelyn S., 27–28
grades, school, 37, 53, 84, 98, 99, 117
Greece, ancient, 6
grief, 47, 103
guidance counselors, school, 38, 52, 61, 64, 68, 79, 80, 83, 86, 118
guilt, 36, 37, 74–75, 77, 78, 89, 98, 103
guns, 14–15, 16, 21–22

hanging, 38, 43, 44, 45, 51, 97, 117
headaches, 54
health issues, 38, 85–86, 89, 106
heavy metal music, 31–32
Helping Hands, 107–109

Index

Hendin, Herbert, 98–99
heredity, 5, 8, 23–24, 31, 32, 39
Hispanic students, 114
homicides, 6
hopelessness, 23, 36, 38, 74, 76, 78, 103
hormones, growth, 25–26
hospitals, 110
hostility, 22, 32, 37
hot lines, 28, 29, 82, 104, 110, 111, 113, 118–119

Illinois, 11, 42
illness:
  self-generated, 85–86
  terminal, 9
Indiana, suicide rate in, 11
insanity, 4, 8
intelligence, 17–18, 49, 51, 65, 66, 67
international organizations, 111–112, 114
Iowa, 87–88, 107
isolation, 22, 23

Japan, suicide rate in, 11
Jersey City, N.J., 84
Joel, Billy, 114
Jones, Michelle, 57–64, 120–121
judgmental responses, 78, 111, 119
jumping, 38, 43

knives, 58, 81, 87

listening, 4, 56, 67–68, 77, 82, 86–87, 101, 108, 111–112, 119
listing good points, 118
loneliness, 38, 108
loners, 45, 51
Los Angeles, Calif., 26, 31
Los Angeles Times, 26
love, 18, 68, 71–72
Lowery, Dick, 88–89
LSD, 29
lymphocytes, 39–40

Manchester, Iowa, 41
manipulation, 18, 76
Mann, John, 25
marijuana, 29
martyrs, 7
Massachusetts, suicide rate in, 11
media coverage, 26–29, 32
mental-health clinics, 110
mental-health specialists, *see* psychologists, psychiatrists, 114–115
Mesa County, Colo., 88
Metropolitan Life Insurance Company, 17
Miami, Fla., 57–64
Michaels, Richard, 29
Michigan, 17
middle-aged people, 33
Mississippi, suicide rate in, 11
moodiness, 36, 98
movies, 27–29
Muscogee County, Ga., 86

music, 31–32, 93, 115
music therapy, 109–110

National Committee on Youth Suicide Prevention (NCYSP), 112–113, 114
National Institute of Mental Health, 24, 33, 35
National-Save-a-Life League, 111
Native Americans, 12, 22
Nature, 39
Nebraska, suicide rate in, 11
Nevada, suicide rate in, 11–12
New England Journal of Medicine, 27
New Jersey, 11, 83–84, 88
New Mexico, suicide rate in, 12
New Providence, Iowa, 107
newspapers, 26–27
New York, N.Y., 17, 27–28
New York Academy of Science, 24
New York State, suicide rate in, 11
911 (emergency number), 82, 110, 118–119
Nora Springs–Rock Falls Junior-Senior High School, 88–89
North Salem, N.Y., 41, 45

Omaha, Neb., 41, 44
operator assistance (0), 82,

operator assistance, *cont'd.*
110, 118–119
organizations, 114–115, 118
Oskaloosa Community Senior High School, 91

parents, 95–102
causes of suicide and, 21, 22–23, 29, 30, 31
communication with, 102
communities and, 105–108
depression and, 33, 34, 37, 38
disruptive behavior and, 13–14, 61, 85, 95–98
expectations and pressures by, 101–102
listening by, 101
potential victim and, 18, 46, 116, 118, 120
professional help sought by, 100–101, 102
schools and, 13, 83, 86, 88, 91, 93, 101, 102
single, 45
suicide as viewed by, 4–5
warning signs and, 49–55
Phillips, David, 26–27
physical complaints, 54
pills, overdose of, 16, 19, 44, 53–54, 55, 58–59, 63, 81, 117
Pittsburgh, University of, 25
Plano, Tex., 45, 88, 110
Plato, 6
Plays for Living series, 104
poison, 18, 49, 68–69

Index

police, 5, 29, 81–82, 110, 115
possessions, giving away of, 16, 52
pregnancy, 12, 13, 20, 37
pressures, 33–34, 37–38, 102, 116
prevention, suicide, 28, 73–121
  by churches and communities, 103–110
  by families, 95–102
  by friends, 73–82
  organizations for, 111–115, 118
  by schools, 83–94
Prinze, Freddie, 27
probation departments, 115
problem solving, 79–80, 84, 119–120
psychologists, psychiatrists, 4, 5, 10, 12–14, 24–31, 38–39, 43, 45, 51, 52, 71, 75, 80, 83, 88, 90, 99, 100, 101, 102, 110, 112, 113, 114–115, 116, 120
Putnam County, N.Y., 41

Quakerdale Home, 107
Quiet Cries, 104–105

record stores, 115
rescue squads, 110
revenge, 21
Richardson, Tex., 41
right-to-die laws, 9

Rockland County, N.Y., 41
rock music, 31–32, 115
romances, 12, 21, 44, 45, 47, 58, 68, 96, 117
Rome, ancient, 6
Romeo and Juliet (Shakespeare), 87
Rosenberg, Mark, 42
Rosenthal, Norman E., 35
Ross, Charlotte, 83, 96–97, 113
Rotheram, Mary Jane, 84–85
Royal Humane Society, 111
runaways, 54, 61–62, 115
Ryan, Neal, 25
Ryerson, Diane, 115

Samaritans, 111–112
San Diego, Calif., 30
San Mateo County, Calif., 96–97
school, schools, 13, 14, 17, 71, 83–94
  and communities, 10, 103–105, 114, 118
  crisis-management programs in, 89–90
  dropouts from, 31, 43, 44, 60, 62, 114, 115
  drugs in, 29, 30
  health-promotion programs in, 85–86, 89
  new students in, 52, 88
  peer-helper groups in, 86–87
  problems in, 33, 51, 54,

school, *cont'd.*
    58, 60, 62, 63, 66–67, 73–74, 115, 120
    suicide-education programs in, 83–84, 88–91
    suicide-prevention measures in, 88–89
    teachers as prevention resource in, 84–85
    weapons in, 87–88
Schools Without Drugs, 29
schoolwork, 53, 56, 86, 120
    see also grades, school
Science Focus, 24
scientific research, 6, 9, 10, 20, 24–31, 39–40
secrecy pledges, 80
self-confidence, 34, 36, 93, 109
self-image, 76
serotonin, 24–25
sexuality, 106, 116
Shaffer, David, 27–28
Shakespeare, William, 87
shame, 4, 15
sharing, 107, 108, 109
shootings, *see* guns
siblings, 59, 60, 65, 67, 68, 69, 95, 97–98, 99
"Silence of the Heart," 28–29
sleeping habits, 35, 53, 98
Smith, Sam (pseudonym), 65–72, 121
social workers, 104, 107
Socrates, 6

solutions, 79, 112, 117–118
South Carolina, suicide rate in, 11
Spencer, Mass., 41
spoken warnings, 55
Stanley, Michael, 25
status, 22, 36
stomachaches, 54
Storm Lake, Iowa, 41, 46
strength, 116–121
stress, 12, 15, 20, 22, 45, 52, 77, 84, 112
    meaningless comparisons and, 37–38
students, new, 52, 88
suffocation, 50
suicidal crisis, 3, 116–117, 118, 120
suicide:
    attitudes about, 3–10
    biochemical markers in, 24–26
    causes of, 4–5, 12–16, 19–32, 37–38, 43, 46–56
    cluster, 41–48, 83, 90, 110
    danger indicators of, 12–14, 75, 96
    decision of, 3, 116–117, 118, 120
    definition of, 5–6
    heredity and, 5, 8, 23–24, 31, 32, 39
    history of, 6–8
    legality of, 5, 6–8, 9
    myths about, 3–5
    nonreporting of, 5, 42

Index

suicide, *cont'd.*
  potential victims of, 11–19
  questions about, 9, 19, 20, 23, 45
  rate of, 11–12
  silence and, 4
  as sin, 7–8, 9
  statistics on, 3–6, 9–12, 14–20, 27, 30, 52, 75–76, 114
  as taboo, 3, 23, 46
  three groups of, 17–19
  victims' profiles in, 14–17
"Suicide in Youth and What You Can Do about It," 114
suicide notes, 17, 58, 65, 68, 89
Suicide Prevention and Crisis Center, 96–97
suicide-prevention centers, 82, 110, 111–115, 119
Sussex, James, 23
Sweden, suicide rate in, 11

talking, 4, 67–68, 76–77, 82, 108, 118, 119
teachers:
  aid and concern of, 69, 71, 83, 95, 120
  causes of suicide and, 29, 30, 31, 46
  in crisis-management programs, 89–90
  disruptive behavior and, 13–14, 58, 62

teachers, *cont'd.*
  in health-promotion programs, 85, 86
  as prevention resource, 84–85, 87, 90, 101, 102
  relationships with, 58, 62, 66, 67, 69, 71, 73, 76
  warning signs and, 49–50, 51, 52, 53
teenagers, 4–5
  birth factors of, 20
  spring as high-risk period for, 103
  statistics on, 4–6, 9–12, 14–17, 20, 75–76, 114
  suicide as viewed by, 4–5
  three groups of, 17–19
  traits of, 20–21, 32, 46
television, 27–29
temper, *see* anger
therapy, 54–55, 79–80, 82, 85, 100–101, 109–110
  see also psychologists, psychiatrists
Three Ds of College, 90–91
Topeka, Kans., 15
trains, 42, 43
"20/20," 31

United States, 11, 111
urban living, 45, 46

Valley View Nursing Home, 107
values, 14, 108
violence, 13, 51, 53–54, 97–98

warning signs, 4, 49–56, 88, 95, 104
  body language, 54–55
  decline in grades or schoolwork, 37, 53, 56, 84, 86, 98, 99, 117, 120
  eating habits, 52, 56, 75, 98
  friends' heeding of, 74–76
  giving away possessions, 16, 52
  physical complaints, 54
  recognition of, 49–52
  running away, 54, 61–62, 115
  sleeping habits, 35, 53, 98
  spoken, 55
  turnaround in behavior, 55–56
  violent or rebellious behavior, 53–54
  withdrawal, 16, 33, 53, 75, 107
Washington, 42
Westchester County, N.Y., 41
withdrawal, 16, 33, 53, 75, 107
worthlessness, 34, 38, 70, 78, 107, 118
wrists, slashing of, 99
Wyoming, 41, 46

Yellow Pages, 110
young adults, 6, 11, 15, 20, 32, 33, 34, 43, 46
Young Women's Christian Association, 105–107
Youth and Family Services, 103, 105
Youth Suicide National Center (YSNC), 83, 87, 113–114

Zerbe, Kathryn, 15

362.2
Fr

Francis, Dorothy B.
Suicide

	DATE DUE		
JAN 2 2 2009			

South Hunterdon Reg. Library
301 Mt. Airy-Harbourton Rd.
Lambertville, NJ 08530